"Since I have saved your life, your life belongs to me."

Tam was confounded, but too frightened to protest. "It does?"

The Shadow nodded ...

"I demand one thing of my agents, Tam: obedience. Absolute, unquestioning obedience."

"You'll have it," Tam said, nodding. "No problem. But tell me one thing, please." He leaned toward The Shadow. "How did you know my life was in danger? Who told you?" Tam caught a glance of piercing, almost reflective eyes.

A trailing, enigmatic laugh issued from the figure in black.

The Shadow knew!

By James Luceno
Published by Del Rey Books:

THE YOUNG INDIANA JONES CHRONICLES, BOOK
ONE: The Mata Hari Affair

A FEARFUL SYMMETRY
ILLEGAL ALIEN
THE BIG EMPTY

Published by Ivy Books:
RIO PASIÓN
RAINCHASER
ROCK BOTTOM

THE
SHADOW

James Luceno

Based on a Screenplay
by David Koepp

IVY BOOKS • NEW YORK

Ivy Books
Published by Ballantine Books
Text and cover art © 1994 Universal City Studios, Inc., and Bregman/Baer Productions, Inc.

The Shadow © Advance Magazine Publishers Inc. The Shadow and associated symbols and word marks are trademarks of Advance Magazine Publishers Inc. Used under license.

Library of Congress Catalog Card Number: 94-96088

ISBN 0-8041-1296-7

Manufactured in the United States of America

First Edition: July 1994

10 9 8 7 6 5 4 3 2 1

For Jim Steranko—artist, author,
acrobat, magician, raconteur—for
keeping me on track.
And for the late Walter Gibson
(aka Maxwell Grant), author extraordinaire,
who could turn out a *Shadow* novel
of this size in five days, on a
Smith-Corona portable.

Acknowledgments

Most of these words belong to David Koepp, though I've also borrowed a phrase here and there from some of the almost three hundred *Shadow* novels written by Walter Gibson throughout the thirties and forties. I've tried to be faithful to both visions.

First and foremost, thanks to my editor, Susan Randol. We were both under the gun, and we made it happen.

And a tip of the slouch hat to those at Bregman/Baer Productions and Universal Studios, who helped me get a sense of what the movie will look like, including Dee Dee, Myron, and David, for showing me the gowns and suits; John Zemansky, for letting me heft the magnums; and Joe Nemec, for the notes and drawings, and for the tour of *Shadow* locations on the back lot.

None of it could have happened without the help of Leona Nevler, of Ivy Books; John Polwrek, of Universal Studios; and Charles O. Glenn, of Bregman/Baer Productions, who opened many a door. And special thanks to Lee Herschman, who went way out of her way.

I am also indebted to Michael Riccardelli, for providing me with *Shadow* comics galore; to Guy Guden, whose *Who Knows What Evil* has recently been published by Graven Images; and to Brian Daley, Karen-Ann, Carmen, Carlos, and Jake, for their unfailing support.

1 A Long Way from Shangri-La

In the fertile river valleys and terraced hillsides that lie in the shadow of Mount Kailasa in western Tibet, the dry season ends in April. By then the wrinkled landscape has taken on a thirsty look, and clearing for spring planting has already commenced. For weeks, axes and machetes have been brought to bear on the thick forest growth above the shrunken rivers, and hundreds of felled trees, dry as kindling, lie about like outsize match sticks. On one auspicious morning, a small army of torch-wielding young men will scurry down the hillsides, setting fire to the trees, leaving in their wake an avalanche of flames that will climb hundreds of feet into the air. Within hours, smoke covers the land, hanging in the valleys like mist and obscuring the sun. But when the smoke clears, the burned fields are blanketed with a fine layer of nurturing ash that has secured the soil's moisture deep within the fire-hardened ground.

Most villages will plant rice or scatter the seeds of other grains, like millet or *gingke*. But a few will court a far more lucrative cash crop: *papaver somnifera*, the delicate opium poppy, which withers and dies in strongly acidic soil and thrives where the substratum is porous and malleable, such as it is in the vicinity of

Kailasa, known in Tibet as Kang Rimpoche, "the great ice jewel."

The hillside palace of the drug lord who reigned over Kailasa gave ample evidence of the benefit that came from opting for the opium poppy. What with its lofty ramparts, precipitous stone walls, and low-pitched roofs of tile and native slate, it soared more than sprawled, dominating the valley whose terraces of white, red, and purple flowers had paid several times over for the embellishments that had come to it: hardwood furniture fashioned in Europe and Japan; carpets from Morocco and Turkestan; fine porcelains from China; silk brocades from southeast Asia; even a gasoline-powered generator transported by airplane from the United States.

Just now those terraces were dotted with harvesters conscripted from several of the local villages. Most wore the sashed tunics or simple blouses and trousers typical of the highland peasantry. The skin of their high-cheekboned faces had a leathery look, and their callused hands held the dull knives used for scraping the gummy black sap from the incised bulbs of the poppy plants. The women wore heavy coral and turquoise necklaces, from which dangled small amulet boxes known as *kaus*. The men kept their hair trimmed short in front and long and braided behind.

Armed with antique breech-loading muskets or with Lee-Enfield rifles that had found their way to Asia from the trenched and shell-cratered post-war landscape of Europe, mounted guards in yak-hide coats and turbanlike headclothes moved menacingly among the workers.

Incongruously, a car horn blared in the heat-shimmered air, and one of the horses reared as a Packard convertible motored into view around a bend in the deeply rutted dirt road that wound up the valley toward the palace. The guard reined in his startled beast and gazed at the late-model automobile with expectant curiosity. Some of the workers stopped to look as well, but any whispered exchanges were immediately silenced. The guard recognized the driver and the figure seated in the rear of the auto, but the man in the passenger seat was unfamiliar. Even so, the man's quilted, cranberry-colored coat and spiked, bronze helmet marked him as a local warload—perhaps from the region of Lake Manasarovar or Parang—and a competitor in the opium trade.

The Packard continued on, its straight-eight power plant sputtering some as the auto gained altitude on the jarring road. The auto crossed a narrow saddle and skidded to a halt in front of the castellated palace, whose principal entrance was flanked by rough-hewn stone sculptures of Fu-dogs, seated forbiddingly on their haunches atop low pedestals.

The driver was a burly Tibetan with a shaved head, flaring eyebrows, and a Fu-Manchu mustache and beard. First out of the Packard, he walked around to the passenger side and threw open the door. "Out," he commanded his helmeted passenger, reaching inside to take hold of him.

"Take your hands from me," Li Peng protested. "Outcast! You dare to touch me?" He was a short but solidly built Chinese, whose left eye had already sustained damage from obviously powerful blows.

Li Peng succeeded in shrugging off the larger man and had a fist cocked when the Tibetan in the rear seat—a long-haired man with a high forehead—drew a foot-long knife from the waistband of his trousers and pressed it to Li Peng's throat.

Momentarily subdued, Li Peng allowed himself to be led away from the car toward the palace's towering front doors, which were painted a garish red-orange and decorated with large bronze strap hinges and knockers.

The doors opened on a stone corridor with a vaulted ceiling. Pressed between the two Tibetans, Li Peng was hauled along at a brisk pace, past dank stairways and fixed-pane windows, then steered to the right into a shorter corridor that ended in an arrowhead arch, filled with lattice-work double doors. The fright Li Peng had experienced on first being abducted had returned, and he began to tremble slightly in the tight grip of his captors.

The room beyond the lattice doors was crowded with ornate furniture, large pillows and sheepskins, inlaid tables, and the low pallets favored by opium smokers. A worn Persian rug, askew to the entry, warmed a portion of the cobblestone floor, and the light from a roaring fire, a lattice-covered skylight, and several table lamps and chandeliers cast a checkerboard of shadows on the walls.

Perhaps a dozen Asian and Western women lounged in studied abandon on the room's slightly elevated upper tier, their faces rouged and their raven hair bunned and braided. Silver and ivory cigarette holders dangled from their slender manicured hands. They wore tattered, tight-fitting Mandarin gowns, beaded flapper dresses, sheer robes, and lingerie. The presence of their stout madam attested to the fact that they were on loan from the brothels of Shanghai or Hong Kong. Interspersed among them reclined Chinese men in silk pajamas and skullcaps, nodded out with their opium pipes, along with a few mysterious-looking Westerners in black suits, who were being ministered to by servants bearing trays of food and wine. The room reeked of cheap perfume, cypress smoke, and the sweet smell of fired opium.

Though much of him was in shadow, the man who had ordered Li Peng snatched from his home on the western shore of Lake Manasarovar was seated at a gilded table on the far side of the room. Sunlight pouring in from a bank of windows behind him made it impossible to see Ying Ko's face. Only his hands were visible: the right, feeding scraps of meat to a bearish, short-haired chow; the left, holding a cigarette. Two armed guards wearing long coats and ear-flapped caps flanked him, and Wu, his chief adviser, was bent over the table, displaying the contents of a large, leather-bound ledger. Three attendants hurried away from the table as the two Tibetans dragged Li Peng forward; otherwise, no one seemed to be paying Li Peng the slightest attention.

The whores' madam started the phonograph, and the strains of big band music began to waver from the machine. The bald Tibetan kowtowed his way out of the room, closing the curved-top doors behind him. Still in the grip of his knife-wielding abductor, Li Peng stood silently in the center of the room, waiting.

Wu closed the ledger, bowed slightly to his employer, and stepped around the table to approach Li Peng, the yard-long book held close to his chest.

"Ying Ko asks too much," Li Peng whispered harshly when Wu was within earshot. "My poppy friends are a glass of water in a rainstorm compared to his. His lips are always moistened with tea or butter, while the rest of us go thirsty."

The hand that had been feeding the dog now held a poppy capsule, which it rolled in a steeplechase over charcoal-smudged knuckles. Ying Ko's fingernails were an inch long and lacquered a dark burgundy. A veil of cigarette smoke drifted lazily in front of him.

Wu compressed his lips. He was an old man, whose sight required the help of round, wire-rim glasses, and whose hairless face bore a mole near the right nostril. He wore a black *p'u-fu* robe with vibrant mandalas embroidered on the front and back, and a round fur cap, whose crown was enlivened by a peacock-feather tassel.

"You and your brothers murdered three of our men," Wu said, as if to remind Li Peng. "We can't let that go unaccounted, can we?"

The captive's whisper grew insistent, and he nodded toward Ying Ko. "He would have done the same if anyone had tried to demand an unfair percentage of the opium trade." Li Peng used the Chinese term, *a-fou-yong*—a rendering of the Arabic *ofium*. "He already controls all the fields below Kang Rimpoche, from the mountain to the lake, and most of the land beyond. The opium trade with Shanghai, Tientsin, Marseilles, and Buenos Aires—it's all his. And as a *philing*—an outlander—he has direct access to both the Corsican crime syndicate and American mafiosi. Everyone knows of his barbaric raid against the tribal chiefs of Barga. Even the Potola in Lhasa isn't sacred to him."

Without warning, he threw off the hand of the guard and took a bold step in Ying Ko's direction. "Send three more and I'll kill them, as well," he warned the shadowed figure.

Ying Ko's filthy hands came to a sudden stop in the room's eldritch light. The poppy capsule was seized in his right hand, and when he opened it nothing was there.

Li Peng martialed his courage. "I'm entitled to my piece," he said, aiming a shaking forefinger at the drug lord. "Kill me if you must, but I promise, my brothers will come for you."

Except for the snap of the fire and the inconstant swirl of the brassy music, the room fell quiet. But at last, and with deadly intent, Ying Ko spoke:

"And I promise you . . . that I will bury them beside you."

In need of a shave and framed by disheveled black hair that fell dully to the tops of broad shoulders, the face that leaned forward into the light had the pale and haggard look of opium addiction. But Ying Ko had a Western face, not more than thirty years in the making, at once captivating and frightening to behold.

Ying Ko directed a casual gesture to his long-haired henchman, and Li Peng immediately felt a hand vice itself on the back of his neck. In the same instant, a glint of firelight off the double-edged blade of the henchman's knife caught his swollen left eye. With the practiced elegance of a trained fighter, Li Peng sent an elbow backward into the Tibetan's solar plexus, even as his right hand was reaching out for the knife. Attempting to come around Li Peng's left side, the guard stepped directly into his captive's backhand and was spun ninety degrees, falling face first to the floor. At the same time, Li Peng—the long knife firmly in hand now—reached out for Wu.

The struggle had lasted only a moment, but Li Peng suddenly had the knife to Wu's throat and was using him as a shield. Revolvers had flashed into view from the waist sashes of Ying Ko's flankers, but neither gunman was positioned for a clear shot. Li Peng could see the prostitutes only peripherally, but their murmurings told him he had their attention.

"I wish only to leave," he announced, his voice raspy with apprehension. "Let me leave."

For emphasis, he pressed the blade to Wu's throat. The old man's palsied hands were clamped on Li Peng's knife hand, though his elbows continued to support the ledger. Throughout, Wu had found amusement in Li Peng's threats—smiling and bobbing his eyebrows—but no longer; Li Peng could hear and feel Wu's labored breathing.

Ying Ko himself had come to his feet. A wool blanket that had covered his lap fell to the floor as he edged around the table and advanced on the stairs. Muscular and over six feet tall, he was barefoot and dressed in a richly embroidered black silk tunic and trousers. His assassins kept their weapons raised but remained where they were. The guard was still facedown on the floor, more, Li Peng surmised, out of humiliation than the force of his backhand.

"I'll cut Wu's throat," he warned. "He's your friend, Ying Ko, your right hand. Even you wouldn't chance seeing him killed."

Ying Ko glanced at the gunmen, calculating something.

"Your men aren't marksmen enough to shoot around him," Li Peng said quickly.

"You're right." Ying Ko answered, his hands at shoulder height in a gesture that begged sensibility. "You're right." Then, looking at Wu with narrowed eyes, he added: "You've been a wonderful friend, Wu."

Wu gasped for breath. "Thank you, Ying Ko."

Ying Ko turned a slow about-face. "Shoot through him," he said to the assassins, plainly delighted to be delivering the unexpected.

The gunmen exchanged smiles.

Li Peng's premature grin faded, and his eyes went wide. He had the knife raised to throw when two shots rang out. The rounds struck the ledger between the large Chinese characters that adorned the cover, ripped through Wu, and tore into Li Peng. Out of concern for their open-toed pumps and fur-topped slippers, the women closest moved their feet to accommodate the fall of the bodies. Rudely awakened from pipe dreams, a black woman with bobbed hair lifted her head in uncertain surprise; others talked quietly among themselves, as if assessing the entertainment value of the deaths.

Ying Ko wore a look of savage excitement. He lifted a brass goblet from his desk and took a long drink; then he raised his arms in the air and uttered a Tibetan phrase that set the entire room laughing. Stepping over the bodies, he walked slowly toward the double doors, appraising the women on his left, some of whom primped for him.

"You," he said, motioning. "And you."

The two stood and followed, one of them belting a white satin robe over her ensemble of black-mesh lingerie. Behind Ying Ko, skullcapped attendants moved in to dispose of the bodies. Almost to the door, the drug lord turned and gestured to a third woman on the other side of the room.

"And you," he said, with a tilt of his chin.

Eurasian, she wore a loose-fitting sheer dress and high-heeled slippers. She had laughed loudest and longest at Ying Ko's joke, but now her painted face fell in arrant dissent. "No," she told her fireplug of a keeper. "I don't want to."

The madam responded by chiding her in Chinese and lashing her with a short-handled, leather-thonged whip.

"All right, I go," the woman said finally. Extricating herself from her gaggle, she hurried for the door, adding her professional sway to the train of flesh Ying Ko was leading from the room.

Night passes quickly in a bed crowded with warm bodies.

Normally, Ying Ko would have ordered a blazing fire built in the bedroom's blackened maw of a fireplace, but that night he had comfort enough on both sides of him, the press of warm skin, the soft caress of fox furs.

The room was a lofty stone perch, with an enormous bed, heavy wooden wardrobes and dressers, and French doors leading to a narrow balcony. Open just now, the doors admitted a cool breeze that stirred diaphanous curtains. Kailasa's shark-fin snowcap hung in the night, an inverted bowl of argent light, and the stars went on forever.

Ying Ko lay on his back, two of the women spooned to his right side, the third to his left. The orbs of his eyes danced wildly under drawn lids, while his mind's eye grappled with a recurring image that had plagued his sleep from the start: that of a teenage Tibetan boy, with shaved skull and serene, though cunning, features.

Ying Ko sat up with a start, sensing that someone was in the room. He listened intently for a moment, then cautiously climbed off the foot of the bed, the women repositioning themselves behind him. He glanced at the balcony and moved toward the center of the room. He hadn't made it halfway when he glanced movement in the crepuscular light.

The meaty fist that caught him on the chin and knocked him unconscious seemed to appear out of no-where.

2 Temple of the Cobras

Consciousness ebbed and waned through indeterminate hours, abetted by a rocking motion that carried him back into vivid dreams each time he neared sleep's liquid surface.

He awoke facing a rising sun to find himself on horseback, his hands bound behind him. The horse was tethered to a lead animal, atop which sat a large Tibetan wearing a fleece-lined longcoat, a short fur cape, an ear-flapped cap, and muddy trousers tucked into knee-high felt boots. When the man turned to give him a look, Ying Ko saw that he had a red scarf pulled up over his mouth and nose. A second man, similarly attired and also powerfully built—the likely owner of the ham-sized fist that had stiffened his jaw—rode nearby.

They were following a narrow trail, lined at intervals with prayer flags and mani walls constructed of flagstones inscribed with the sacred Buddhist mantra: *Om mani padme hum*. In the near distance, Ying Ko could discern the pinnacle top of a large stupa.

He was wearing his black silk trousers, and someone had thrown a black goat hide over his bare shoulders. The coppery taste of blood lingered in his mouth, and his wrists had been chafed by the rope.

"Are you Li Peng's brothers?" he asked in Mandarin. "Or do you simply belong to him?"

The rider beside him seemed to grin, and shook his head as if to say, you should be so lucky.

Ying Ko shrugged it off. Perhaps they were no more than thieves. Drawing pilgrims as it did, the Kailasa region was notorious for the robbers that preyed on them. Either way, he was impressed. Only capable agents could have infiltrated the palace and spirited him from it unseen. Or had there been a gunfight as well?

"Where are you taking me?" he asked.

The same rider nodded in the direction of Kailasa.

Ying Ko assessed his surroundings. The thin air told him that they had climbed several thousand feet above the valley floor and the road that ringed the mountain, along which pilgrims performed their circuit of prostrations.

"A *tulku* wishes to see you," the rider added after a long moment.

Ying Ko raised an eyebrow. The term referred to a lama of supreme rank—a living Buddha. "A holy man wants to see me?" He laughed heartily. "I think you're going to find out you grabbed the wrong guy." He laughed and settled in for the ride.

Hours passed. The trail switchbacked higher up the slopes toward the tree line, gradually leveling out as it closed in on a sheer rock wall that buttressed the southern flanks of the sacred mountain itself. The area was strewn with elaborate stupas and chortens, and a profusion of prayer flags snapped in the wind. The only structure that might have served as a home, however, was a simple wattle-and-daub goat herder's hut, centered in a grouping of stone corrals. A far cry from the monastery Ying Ko had been imagining.

"Nice *gompa*," he said when the horses had stopped. "Or maybe you meant to say that a *hermit* wanted to see me."

The Tibetan riders dismounted. One of them helped Ying Ko down. He was still regarding the hut with a look of bemusement when the Tibetan nearest him shook his head and said, "No. There."

Ying Ko followed the man's finger to the sheer wall, astonished to see a lamasery shimmer into visibility. Modeled on Lhasa's Potola, its manifold roofs were four-hipped and its towering white walls were dimpled with scores of narrow windows. Though unlike the Potola, the main entrance lay deep within the open mouth of an immense cobra, whose hood alone had to be fifty feet wide.

Ying Ko's own mouth had fallen open. He cut his eyes to the Tibetans.

"The clouded mind sees nothing," one of the men answered through his scarf.

Roughly, they escorted him to the mouth's sculpted tongue, where they stripped him of the goat's hair cape and flung him toward a pair of Brobdingnagian doors, which rose between snarling bronze lions. Eighteen feet high, the doors were studded with plate-sized gold lozenges, and their outsize vertical handles appeared to have been carved from the thigh bones of a brontosaurus. From behind them came the slow, almost funereal beat of kettle drums.

Pulled by unseen hands, the door opened inward, revealing a long room that ended in a canopied, golden altar, surmounted by effulgent golden curtains. Two rows of painted columns supported the room's central nave, from the ceiling of which hung short, square-cut crimson and gold banners. Paralleling the colonnades stood two lines of monks, each man wearing a drum at chest height and holding a wooden beater. The lamas wore saffron and crimson robes and ceremonial head-dresses topped by tall Mohawks of mustard-colored napping. Several bare-headed acolytes faced Ying Ko from the foot of the altar, some holding silver bells, two with their mouths pressed to eight-foot-long *ragdong* trumpets, whose sound boxes rested on the gilded floor. None of them acknowledged Ying Ko as he approached the altar, but when he was within a few feet of it, the plangent drumming ceased on a double strike, the bells sounded, and the lamas turned without word and disappeared behind the columns.

Ying Ko regarded the altar with stifled awe. Golden cobras spiraled around the canopy's forward support posts, and on the floor were several small, golden tables, replete with ritual objects. But Ying Ko's attention was fixed on the translucent curtain that hung over the three-foot-high altar, rippling in a breeze he couldn't feel. Behind it, a large golden disk could be distinguished, and emerging from that disk—as if levitated above the altar—was the form of a human figure seated in a lotus position.

The seated figure was a young boy, clothed in robes that blended impeccably with the sumptuousness of his surroundings. He had narrow eyes, a wide nose, and full lips. Small bumps along the forehead were all that marred a cleanly shaved skull. Ying Ko's dream from the previous night returned with unsettling swiftness as the youth seemed to float toward him.

"Who are you?" Ying Ko demanded in Tibetan, only to be answered in English.

"I am Marpa Tulku," the boy said. "You recognize me."

It wasn't a question, but Ying Ko denied the assertion. "I've never seen you before." He brushed strands of hair from his face.

The boy's face betrayed nothing. "You have seen me—as pictures in your mind. I am your teacher."

Ying Ko gaped at him in amused disbelief. "My what?"

"Your teacher. You have been chosen."

"Chosen for what?"

"You will see."

Ying Ko sneered. "Like I told your pals, you've made a serious mistake."

"There is no mistake."

Ying Ko's hands brushed at the dusty thighs and knees of his loose trousers. "Do you have any *idea* who you've kidnapped?"

"Cranston," the boy said.

Ying Ko froze. Cranston wasn't his real name, though it was the name he had arrived in Tibet wearing. When he looked up, the *tulku* was standing directly in front of him.

"Lamont Cranston," the boy said.

Ying Ko forced a fearless grin and touched his hirsute chest. "So you know my real moniker."

"I also know that for as long as you can remember you've struggled against your own black heart, and that you have always lost the battle." The boy was circling him now, gazing at him—through him, it seemed. "You've watched your spirit, your very face change when the beast claws its way from inside you. You are in great pain, aren't you?"

Cranston bristled. "I'll show you pain—"

He made a sudden lunge for the youth but found only thin air. In startled amazement, he lurched off balance toward the altar.

"You know what evil lurks in the hearts of men, because you've glimpsed that evil in your own heart. That makes you a powerful man, Lamont Cranston. But I intend to make you more powerful still."

The *tulku*'s voice came from somewhere behind Cranston. He turned, spied the boy standing near one of the columns, and made another leap for him, this one carrying him clear into a side room, with nothing to show for it but abraded elbows from landing face first on the hard floor.

"Some holy man," Cranston said, getting up. "You're nothing but a *naljorpa*—a sorcerer."

"I am an insect fluttering in the dung," came the youth's disembodied voice. "I roll in the dung like a pig. I digest it and fashion it into gold dust, into a brook of pure water, into stars. To fashion stars out of dog dung, is that not great work?"

"What've I got to do with stars?" Cranston asked, circling warily, trying to close on the voice.

The boy laughed. "Nothing. But you have much in common with dog dung."

Seeing him reappear near the column, Cranston threw himself through the air, tumbling down into the main room once more.

"Your redemption could require a year, perhaps longer. But I will teach you to use your black shadow to battle evil in place of fomenting it. Every one pays a price for redemption."

The *tulku* materialized right next to Cranston and just as quickly faded from view.

"—this is yours."

Shivering with fear, Cranston backed away on his hands and feet. "I'm not looking for redemption."

A chilling laugh filled the room.

" 'The ocean does not resent too much water, nor does the treasury resent too much treasure. The people do not resent too much wealth, and the wise do not resent too much knowledge.' " The boy paused. "You have no choice. You *will* be redeemed."

A shadow thrown by an invisible figure crawled across the floor toward Cranston, rising above him on the resplendently curtained wall above the altar.

By now, he had effectively backed himself into a corner. But alongside him on a low table, resting horizontally atop two triangular bases, lay a *phurba*—an elongated ritual dagger used by magicians, with pointed blades that spread into a triangle up to the hilt.

The *tulku* divined his intent. "I wouldn't do that. That dagger has been the property of many powerful men over the centuries, and in it resides their combined strengths."

"I'll take my chances," Cranston said, grinning and taking hold of the bayonetlike dagger. He scampered to his feet and began to stalk his invisible prey.

The knob of the knife's handle was an exquisitely carved head wearing a crown. The face centered in the head was Asiatic and somewhat barbaric-looking, though the carving's real power lay in its lifelike quality. In fact, the more Cranston stared at it, the more lifelike it seemed to become. Worse, the thing was suddenly vibrating in his grip, as if unhappy with its situation. When it started to spin in his hand, Cranston glanced down at it in time to see the now snarling face sink teeth into the fleshy base of his thumb.

He yelped and let go of the handle, nursing his hand while he watched the dagger hit the floor on its tip and skitter to the center of the room. He made a quick dive for it, but it scurried away and launched itself into the air. There it executed a series of spins and rotations, and dove for him, embedding itself an inch deep into the top of his left thigh.

Screaming in pain, Cranston collapsed on his rear and yanked the knife from his raggedly torn flesh. Only the strength of both hands prevented the knife from striking him in the groin. Instead, it hit the floor point first, then bounded up out of his grip, hovered for a moment, and flew toward his face.

A veteran of numerous dogfights with *Boche* pilots in the skies over France during the Great War, Cranston had never come up against anything like the *phurba*.

Just in time, he jerked his head to one side. The dagger glanced off a column and went swooping through the room, ricocheting off columns and crashing into one of the incense stands below the altar. Cranston was flattened against the room's rear wall when the blade got him in its sights again. Then it plummeted, only to stop inches from his face and hover there for a moment to glare at him. Finally it rocketed forward, darting about his face like the trained bullwhip of a circus performer, striking the wall left, right, and above his head. Reversing course, it doubled up in a right angle to show a vicious snarl before streaking toward him, spinning end over end.

The triangular blade grazed Cranston's cheek, opening a razorlike wound, then soared behind his head and shot for the altar, into the waiting grip of the suddenly remanifested *tulku*.

The hilt face returned to bronze as Cranston slid weakly to the floor, clutching his bleeding thigh.

"He who knows how could live comfortably in hell," the boy told him.

"Is that where I am?" Cranston asked in a pained whisper. "In hell?"

The *tulku* smiled lightly. "Not yet."

And the doors to the room slammed shut.

3 The Shadow Strikes!

Forcibly apprenticed to the *tulku*, time stood still for the man who answered to the names Ying Ko and Lamont Cranston, but time marched on for the rest of the world.

The stock market crashed, ushering in the Great Depression; Hitler and the Nazi Party rose to power in Germany; the planet Pluto was discovered; talkies replaced silents, and American audiences saw their first musical Mickey Mouse cartoons; in New York City, the Empire State Building was dedicated; the Graf Zeppelin airship circled the globe in twenty days; the words neoprene, nylon, and neutron were introduced to the English language; the first aircraft carrier was launched; electronic television was developed; the U.S. Marines left Haiti; the first all-star game was played; Prohibition was ended; and Alcoholics Anonymous was organized.

But even after seven years of world-shaking events, some things remained constant: Coca-Cola was still the most popular soft drink and racketeers were still a force to be reckoned with in American life, especially in New York City, where Scarface Capone's imprisonment for tax evasion had created a vacuum that had to be filled.

Duke Rollins figured he was just the one to fill Big Al's shoes. He had a mind for the business, and he had an eye for the dames. What's more, he was good with guns, and he wasn't afraid to use them. Crossed, he responded in kind, no matter if the double-dealer was a copper or some mobbie stooge. Sometimes it was neither; just some mug who saw something he wasn't supposed to see. But even then you did what you had to do. A rubout was a rubout, and had to be handled properly.

Tonight's, for instance. Some guys might have been tempted to let the Chinese walk, even after what he'd seen. But Duke knew better than to leave himself wide open to face a murder rap. So he'd had the Chinese snatched and fitted for galoshes. But, hey, at least Duke would be seeing to the farewell in person. More than you could say about a lot of mugs.

Owing to the lateness of the hour, the rain, or maybe the thick fog, the Harlem River Bridge connecting the South Bronx to Manhattan was deserted. Not that Duke would have been troubled by a passing car or two, but you never looked a gift horse in the mouth. So he was smiling to himself when he pulled the Ford sedan to the curb on the Manhattan-bound lane of the bridge and stepped out to have a closer look at the cold waters of the Harlem River.

English Johnny climbed out from the rear seat to join him. Both men wore dark, woolen trenchcoats and snap-brimmed trilbys. The larger of the two, Duke had a humorless face, accented by a neatly trimmed mustache. Johnny's face had been ravaged by the pox, and his chin was dimpled.

Duke blew into his hands to warm them as he peered into the fog beneath the bridge, trying to make out the water. If nothing else, he could tell the river was choppy, from the slapping sound of the water against the pylon piers.

"I hate bridges," Johnny commented around a cigarette.

"So what? We won't be here long." Duke shoved the wooden end of a match stick into his mouth and gestured with his head to the black sedan. "Get the Chinee."

The rear door on the driver's side swung open as Johnny was approaching. Maxie, also sporting trenchcoat and trilby, stepped out and hurried around to the opposite side of the car, throwing open the rear door.

"Out you go, Dr. Tam," Maxie said, poking his head in. Johnny leaned in alongside of him to lend a hand.

"I didn't see anything," Tam yelled in a frightened, thinly accented voice. "I swear, I didn't see anything."

"Pipe down, mug," Maxie told him. "This won't hurt . . . much."

Tam's efforts to resist proved futile. The two mobbies dragged him headfirst from the rear seat and hauled him to his feet. Late thirties, Tam was clean-shaven and wearing a simple glen plaid single-breasted suit and bow tie. He wasn't a large man, but he made for an unwieldy package that night.

"Is it dry?" Duke shouted from the railing.

Maxie produced a stiletto from the pocket of his trenchcoat, leaned down, and poked at the rectangular block of concrete that encased Tam's feet to the ankles. "Perfect, Duke," he called back.

"Then bring him over . . . and try not to ruin his new shoes."

The two partners in crime grabbed the Asian under the arms and dragged him to the railing.

"I'll never tell anyone," Tam said in a panic. "I swear."

Johnny was grinning. "That's a sure bet, boyo."

When Tam's back was to the rail, Duke stepped in close to study him, still chewing on the match stick.

"Wish I could trust you, I really do. But you picked the wrong alley to look down. Call it bad luck."

Tam's eyes were wide pools of black. "Please, I'm begging you. I have a family."

"So figure we're doin' ya a favor," Maxie said.

Johnny nodded in transparent concern. "Besides, they'll get over it."

Tam shook his head back and forth. "I won't talk."

"Save it," Johnny said.

Duke took the match from his mouth and executed one of his favorite sleight-of-hand routines, running the head of the match through Tam's thick black hair while igniting the thing with his thumbnail. He held the lighted match in front of Tam's face. "I know you won't talk." Cutting his eyes to Johnny and Maxie, he added, "Dump him," and blew out the match.

Tam screamed as the two mobbies began to bend him backward over the top of the railing. His hands clutched wildly at the wide lapels of their coats.

"I hate manual labor," Johnny said, grunting.

"Then let's just show 'im across and be done with it."

They had Tam a foot off the pedestrian walkway when a resonant peal of laughter sounded through the fog. Duke's henchmen froze and traded spooked looks. Even Tam ceased his struggling for a moment.

"Cripes, what gives with that?" Maxie asked.

The laugh returned, mocking now, seeming to issue from every direction.

Duke's hand plunged into his coat and reappeared holding a snub-nosed revolver. "Who's there? Show yourself, mug, or I'll give it to you good."

A deep, sinister voice broke the silence. "You murdered a policeman, Duke."

Johnny and Maxie showed their weapons—a .38 and a .45—and threw mad glances toward the car, the bridge tower, the fog itself. "Who said that?" Maxie managed. "Duke, who's saying that?"

Duke glared at him. "Shut your trap."

The voice intoned: "The weed of crime bears bitter fruit, Duke. Crime does not pay."

Once more, Maxie swung on Duke. "This ain't good, this ain't good, at all. Diamond Bert and Flash Gidley told me they heard of a couple of mugs got tagged by some bird at the South Street piers, and they couldn't even see him!"

Duke worked his jaw. "I said, shut your clam. I heard that story, and I'll tell you what I think. I think Bert and Flash are off their nuts, see? They've been smoking dope, get it? This guy's no phantom, and I'll prove it." He strode past the nose of the sedan, out into the center of the bridge.

The phantom's response was a contemptuous laugh. "Did you think you'd get away with it, Duke? Did you think *I* wouldn't know?"

Duke spun around, digging a finger into his ear and searching for the source of the voice. "Think you're pretty smart, don't you. Well, take this—"

The snub-nose barked as Duke turned through a three-quarter circle, sending rounds high and low into the swirling fog. Behind him, Maxie, Johnny, and the immobile Tam crouched in apprehension.

The phantom's trailing laugh now seemed to come from the Bronx side of the bridge. Duke stormed past the car and emptied his gun into the air.

"I could easily answer you in kind, Duke. But I want you alive." The voice was a perfect imitation of Duke's.

Rollins fumed, rushing to the passenger side of the Ford and pulling a tommy gun from the open rear. He returned to the center of the bridge and loosed an extended volley, spinning through a full circle, laughing wildly while the chatterbox riddled the night air. Johnny and Maxie ducked for cover as the Thompson's rounds shattered lamppost globes, sconces mounted on the tower, even the side windows of the Ford. Duke stormed to the railing and fired another ricocheting burst into the pedestrian tunnel that ran through the pylon. The gun smoked and spit spent cartridges onto the pavement and the walkway.

When it was over, the cooling tommy pinging in the breathless silence, Maxie poked his head cautiously from behind the hood of the car. "You think you got him, Duke?"

Rollins returned an assured chuckle. "Does a dog have fleas? You're goddamn right I—"

Duke's head snapped back as though punched, and he pitched forward to the rain-slicked pavement, losing the submachine gun. He moaned and lifted his head, fingering a bloody nose.

Maxie stared at him in alarm. "Duke, Duke, you're giving me the willies, throwing yourself to the ground like that."

Panting, Duke scrambled to his feet, raising his fists

like a prize fighter and turning in a circle, trying to draw a bead on his unseen assailant. "Show yourself, you yellow-bellied—"

Duke doubled over, clutching his stomach; then his head snapped back once more and something propelled him headfirst into the railing. Maxie, Johnny, and Tam watched mutely as Duke's trenchcoat bunched up around his neck and he was hoisted off his feet by some invisible force. The polished toes of his shoes performed an anxious shuffle on the walkway, and Duke's face began to turn purple in the eerie glow of the street lamps.

"You committed murder, Duke," the baleful voice told him. "Now you're going to confess to your crime."

Out came a tooth with Duke's mouthful of blood. "That's a lie, screw. You're all wet."

He might have had something to add, but just then the force heaved him ten feet through the air to the center of the bridge, where he landed in a heap among the tommy's shell casings. When he managed to get to his feet, he was snorting for breath through a broken nose, and the trilby was gone, exposing the bald pate that was the bane of his existence.

"I'm not confessing to nothing!"

"You will, Duke," the phantom countered. "Because if you don't, I'll be there—around every corner, in every empty room—as inevitable as a guilty conscience."

Duke took a series of punches to the face and body before being thrown against the left front fender of the car; then over it to the walkway, close to where Tam was cowering; then over the railing itself, only to hang suspended in the air.

"Don't force me to act as your judge and jury,

Duke," the voice warned. "I don't believe in the death penalty. I *am* the death penalty."

Duke was hanging upside-down over the water, as if being dangled by his left foot, the trenchcoat cascading down over his jerking arms and head.

"I'll finish you right here," the voice promised. "I'll plant you where you intended to plant him."

Blood dripping from his mouth and nose, Duke could hear and smell the salt chop of the water. The fight had gone out of him, and fear had reared up in its place. "Okay, okay, you got me dead to rights. I'll do what you say. I'll confess. Just don't let me fall, don't let me fall." He was whimpering like a baby.

The phantom's retort was a snort of derisive laughter. "You will go to the Eighth Precinct House on Second Avenue, and there you will surrender yourself to Desk Sergeant Noonan. And you will do it tonight."

The same unseen hands that had thrown Duke over the rail suddenly hoisted him back onto the walkway, only to toss him headfirst across the hood of the Ford, and directly through the split windscreen.

Maxie and Johnny still had their weapons out and their mouths open. They wanted no part of Duke's problem and were backing away when a shadow appeared on the pavement, elongating in their direction until it finally encompassed and rose over them, high on the tower. Two pairs of terrified eyes followed the shadow to its source, where a parcel of the befogged darkness resolved into the profile of a human figure. The figure topped six feet and was cloaked in black from shoes to wide-brimmed hat, which was pulled low on its forehead. What little could be seen of its face behind a red scarf was fierce-eyed and hawklike, and around him the cloak fluttered and snapped like some animate creature of the night.

His laugh sibilant and bone-chilling, The Shadow swirled forward like a dark-stained portion of the fog itself.

"I hate this guy," Johnny stammered, before he and Maxie turned tail and ran toward the lights of Manhattan.

The Shadow watched them go, then glided around the car to confront Tam, who was shaking like a leaf and rocking back and forth on his own concrete pier.

"Please," he said, "I-I didn't see anything—"

The Shadow whipped back his cloak, revealing the butts of shoulder-holstered automatics. He crossed black-gloved hands over his chest and drew the twin weapons, aiming them down at Tam. On the third finger of the left hand glowed a large red stone in a silver ring.

Tam knew a little about guns, and he saw now that what he had first taken for .45 Colts were heftier, nickel-plated handguns with mother-of-pearl handles. It took strong wrists and powerful forearms to control such weapons, but The Shadow's were more than equal to the challenge.

Tam squeezed his eyes shut. Instantly, the air around him rang with eight explosive shots, and his feet seemed to leap from their shell of imprisoning concrete. In the subsequent silence, he glanced down at his legs fully expecting to find that his feet had been blown off, but realizing instead that the black-clad avenger's bullets had chunked the block, freeing him.

Tam stared at the narrow-eyed man in the cloak, scarf, and hat. "Who are you?"

But before the question could be answered a taxicab

tore out of the fog and screeched to a halt alongside the mobsters' Ford, out of which protruded The Shadow's still unconscious foeman, Duke Rollins. Like the guns, the taxi was like no other Tam had encountered around town, but rather a late-model, yellow and black, front-wheel-drive Cord touring sedan, somewhat longer than the standard model, with wide whitewalls, headlamps that rotated outward from compartments in the bulbous front fenders, and exhaust pipes jutting from both sides of the hood. On the roof was a trio of yellow Moderne running lights in the form of rising suns, with the words "Sunshine Radio" below the center light.

The rear door of the taxi opened of its own accord. The Shadow extended a hand to Tam and motioned him to enter. Tam did so, sliding all the way to the left, dismayed to learn that The Shadow planned to follow him in.

The door closed and the hack squealed into the night.

"Drive, Shrevvy," The Shadow had instructed the hackie.

The name on the license was Moe Shrevnitz. From behind, in peacoat and tweed hat, he looked fifty or so. He drove daringly, with one arm thrown over the front seat, throwing glances to the backseat, taking every turn at the highest possible speed, scarcely looking at the road. The rates stenciled on the front doors of the cab were twenty cents for the first quarter mile, five cents additional, but, while the on-duty lights were lit, the cab's black meter box was silent.

Tam risked a slight turn toward his backseat companion while Shrevnitz was barreling the cab south, along Manhattan's East Side. He had no idea where he was being taken.

Only a portion of The Shadow's aquiline profile was visible between the brim of the black hat and the scarlet scarf and upturned collar of the black, double-breasted frock coat he wore underneath the wool cloak. Aware of Tam's gaze, The Shadow tugged his sleeve down over his right hand; the glove had been removed, and his hand was cut and bloodied from the beating he had meted out to Duke Rollins.

"Thank you," Tam said at last. "For saving me." When The Shadow didn't respond, he looked to the chauffer. "Uh, you fellows are probably busy, so you can just drop me anywhere along the—"

"You're Dr. Roy Tam," The Shadow interrupted, his voice deep and susurrant. "A professor in the science department at New York University. A metallurgist, I believe."

"Yes," Tam said, amazed. "But how—"

"A theoretical physicist in your native country, a metallurgist here." The Shadow snorted. "I've known of you for some time, Dr. Tam, and have long considered recruiting you."

Tam showed him a puzzled look. "Recru—"

"I know, too, that you witnessed something two nights ago that almost got you killed tonight. Fortunately, I was made aware of Duke Rollins's plans for you and was on hand to save you." The Shadow looked at him out of the corner of his eye. His eyebrows were as bushy as caterpillars. "Your gratitude is appreciated, but it's not enough. Since I have saved you life, your life belongs to me."

Tam was confounded but too frightened to protest. "It does?"

The Shadow nodded. "You will become my agent—

like dozens of others all over the world, in all walks of life. Some carry out missions for me every day, others may carry out only one in their lifetime. But theirs are lives with purpose, Dr. Tam. Purpose and honor." He turned slightly toward Tam, as if waiting for a response.

Tam gulped and found his voice, opting for humor, his best defense. "Could I, uh . . . ask my wife about this?"

"No," The Shadow told him sternly.

"Okay." He swallowed audibly, telling himself: no jokes. A sudden right turn threw him against the door. Shrevnitz drove as if there were no tomorrow.

"Your life will proceed as always," The Shadow said. "Mr. Shrevnitz will instruct you in the way in which you will be contacted should I ever require your help. When you hear one of my agents say, 'The sun is shining,' you will respond, 'But the ice is slippery.' This will identify you to each other. Do you understand?"

" 'The sun is shining'?"

"But the ice is slippery."

Tam mulled it over for a moment, wondering suddenly if the joke wasn't on him. "What then?"

"You will await my instructions." The Shadow paused briefly. "I demand one thing of my agents, Tam: obedience. Absolute, unquestioning obedience."

"You'll have it," Tam said, nodding. "No problem. But tell me one thing, please." He leaned toward The Shadow. "How did you know my life was in danger? Who told you?" Tam caught a glance of piercing, almost reflective eyes.

A trailing, enigmatic laugh issued from the figure in black.

The Shadow knew!

4 The Shadow Masked

Shrevnitz threw the Cord into a screeching right-hand turn, but drove for only a block under the elevated train line before making another right and pulling over to the curb on the wrong side of the street. Manhattan was wet, but the temperature had actually nosed up a couple of degrees. Tam, still shaken from his brush with death and the white-knuckle ride from the Harlem River Bridge, understood that he was expected to take the subway home, and wasted no time scrambling out onto the sidewalk. Shrevnitz exited as well, from the Cord's rear-hinged driver's door. Tam's black-clad rescuer remained in the cab.

Tam said thank you as he hurried out, then turned to Shrevnitz in agitated excitement, gesturing to the backseat as the hackie led him away from the car.

"That's The Shadow. I mean, *that's* The Shadow. . . ."

Shrevnitz took hold of Tam's right hand and began to pump it, humoring him with a nod and a grin. "Hey, you're a pretty smart guy."

He was a tall man, with large features and mischievous eyes. Beneath the peacoat he wore a flannel shirt and dark-green wide-wale corduroys.

Tam was still peering at the rear window of the cab. "I've heard the rumors on the radio and read them in the papers, but I thought it was just talk. I didn't think he existed."

"He doesn't, get it?" Shrevnitz's eyes narrowed, and he touched a forefinger to his temple.

Tam returned a blank stare, then a slow nod of comprehension. More of that agent business, he told himself. But what did it mean to be an agent of The Shadow's? The hackie had released his hand, but there was something on it that hadn't been there before: a heavy silver ring, adorned with a smooth oval of ruby-red stone. Slipped onto his third finger, where some American men wore wedding rings.

"Don't ever take it off," Shrevnitz cautioned. He winked and turned to go when Tam took hold of his arm.

"Wait a minute. Who are you? What part do you play in all this?"

"Somebody who owes him his life." Shrevnitz's eyes bored in on Tam, and he raised his right hand, displaying an identical ring. "Someone just like you," he added, jabbing Tam lightly in the chest.

Tam was still standing on the sidewalk, wondering how he was going to explain the ring to his wife, when the taxi sped off.

Shrevnitz continued downtown at a more subdued pace. He had both hands on the steering wheel now and faced forward in the seat. Every so often he allowed his eyes to drift toward the rearview mirror, not, however, to check on traffic but to check on his passenger, who sat like a lump of solid darkness in the backseat. The Shadow's rapid breathing could be heard over the noise of the engine and gearbox. More, there was a strong smell of astringent in the air.

"You okay, boss?" he asked.

"Nothing that won't mend," The Shadow told him after a long moment.

Shrevnitz heard the sound of the drawer opening—a secret compartment one of The Shadow's agents, Chance Labrue, had installed under the rear seat when he'd added two feet to the overall length of the car. The drawer concealed clothes of all sorts, makeup kits, medical supplies, clips of ammunition, an assortment of wigs and mustaches, false noses, and cauliflower ears. The Shadow was stirring now, visible in the rearview, as the hat, cloak, and jacket came off, to be stored for future use.

Shrevnitz thought about Roy Tam, and about his own first encounter with The Shadow, five years earlier. Tam would be surprised to learn the extent of the secret fraternity into which he had been enlisted. A fraternity whose New York chapter alone included the clean-cut Harry Vincent; Clyde Burke, now a staff reporter for *The Classic*; "Cliff Marsland," who moved effortlessly among the city's gangsters and racketeers; Rutledge Mann—the network's "man"—who headed up The Shadow's intelligence bureau; Hawkeye, the stoop-shouldered panhandler; Jericho Druke, a black of unsurpassed strength; Tapper, Stanley, Yat Soon, Dr. Rupert Sayre . . . the list went on and on.

Shrevnitz had worked with all of them over the years, and in all kinds of circumstances. Duke Rollins obviously considered himself a tough guy, but he was small potatoes compared to some The Shadow had taken on; archfiends of crookdom, like Mox, Macmurdo, Q, the

Green Terror, the Vindicator, and Rodil, who called himself Doctor Mocquino ... Another list that went on and on.

Shrevnitz heard the drawer close and glanced at the rearview mirror. The Shadow had moved to the center of the seat and was leaning forward. In the light of the street lamps and the dashboard gauges, he looked fatigued, either from his efforts on the bridge or from the feverish excitation his violent encounters frequently gave rise to. But he was dressed for a different form of nightlife now, in tuxedo, black overcoat, and white scarf. His thick black hair was combed straight back, and the relaxed muscles of his face had assembled themselves into the handsome features of Lamont Cranston. The ring, adjusted to fit his bare finger, shone from his left hand.

"The usual place, Mr. Cranston, sir?"

The transformed Shadow nodded.

The Cobalt Club was near Times Square, in among the theaters, private clubs, swell shops, and fancy restaurants. The Cobalt itself had once been an exclusive men's club, but those days were gone. Now it was the latest epicenter of the city's social scene, a place to see and be seen. A fiend known as the Black Tiger had even declared war on the club a couple of years back, but The Shadow had put a quick end to that. Lamont Cranston had been a member in good standing for close to ten years, and he was known by the waiters to be the best tip on the block.

The round-topped entrance was as elegant as the interior was rumored to be, featuring a square of Modernistic canopy that supported the club's name done in white neon block letters, and under which stood eager-to-please doormen in top hats, braid, and cobalt-blue jackets.

As Cranston entered—the doormen tipping their hats and the coat-check girl giving him her best smile—he stowed his pain where it couldn't get at him. The hand that had made mincemeat of Duke Rollins's face was feeling better, makeup covering what he hadn't been able to heal through a *tumo* summoning, which brought body heat to a wounded area. His mentor Marpa Tulku had been able to stick pins through his tongue, sleep atop the sharpened edges of swords, stride with impunity over hot coals, send messages on the wind, render himself seemingly invisible, subsist on a diet of edible fungi, endure subzero temperatures, walk for endless hours without rest on the Tibetan plateau. . . . But only a few of those uncanny abilities had been successfully communicated to his fretful student.

Cranston paused at the top of a short stairway to survey the club's main room. Wainwright Barth was seated at his customary table on the far side of the room, far enough from the band so that the waiters could take his order without having to lean over with hands to their ears.

The room was equal parts Hollywood and Buck Rogers, with square tables arranged on either side of a gleaming dance floor. Behind the raised level where the band sat rose a towering fan of gold lamé, down the center of which ran a stripe of shimmering cobalt-blue fabric that might as well have been made of feathers plucked from some exotic jungle bird. The intense blue was picked up in the glass panels of a stately pillar that stood at the center of a rectangular bar that took up a corner of the room. Elsewhere were embossed wall panels that shone like silver, etched-glass windows, tall porcelain urns, and glittering chandeliers and sconces. The club demonstrated its progressiveness by featuring an integrated band, fronted by a buxom, black female singer, who usually wore her hair in a bun and that night was wearing a blue halter dress.

Cranston eyed Barth's table once more. The nearly empty plates meant that Barth had gotten tired of waiting for his erstwhile, gadabout nephew and gone ahead and eaten. Cranston gave a smart tug to his Saville Row jacket and crossed the room, greeting regulars in route and signaling a waiter to bring him the usual. Many of them knew him as "Monty."

"Sorry I'm late, Uncle Wainwright," he said, settling himself into the straight-backed chair opposite Barth's. "There was an accident on the bridge."

Barth grunted resentfully and continued to mop up what was left of his meal. He was a large man with a big, round head and the soulful eyes of a hound dog in a fleshy face. His salt-and-pepper hair was neatly combed, and the lapel of his crisply tailored tuxedo jacket sported a white carnation. A member of the gentry, or so it would seem; but, in fact, he was the city's newest police commissioner.

"I didn't think you'd want me to wait," Barth said finally, in between bites. "The prime rib is excellent, by the way."

A waiter appeared with two martinis and placed them in front of Cranston.

"Your usual, Mr. Cranston."

Cranston thanked him, popped one of the olives into his mouth, and took a long sip from the fluted glass. Alcohol wreaked havoc on the body, but it was important to keep up appearances.

Barth set his fork down and dabbed at his mouth with a linen napkin. "I'm very upset with you, Lamont."

Cranston sighed on cue and took another sip. "What is it this time?"

"Mr. Hadley Richardson is one of New York's most respected financial counselors. I had to pull a lot of strings to get you that meeting with him. You could have at least had the decency to hear him out."

"I got caught up," Cranston said, angling away from the table, his eyes sweeping the room for something of interest.

Barth reddened. "You got caught up. Too damn busy to meet with Mr. Hadley Richardson?"

Cranston made no reply. A young woman stood at the top of the stairs, gazing about as he had earlier. Attractive without having had to resort to the serene, languid look of the moment, she had a curvaceous if slender figure and a bonnet of wavy, golden-blond hair that barely reached her ivory-white shoulders. Cranston waited to see if she had arrived unescorted.

Her gown was cream satin and hugged her like paint. It had an array of crystal-fringed sashes that crisscrossed her breasts and dangled over one shoulder, secured by a silver brooch. An actress, Cranston thought, as the maître d' was showing her to a table. Half the men in the room were oogling her, but she was ignoring the attention, as only someone accustomed to attention could do.

One man, who had the look of a tennis pro, was waving and grinning at her, showing perfect teeth. The woman acknowledged him with a tight smile and a gesture that anyone smart enough would have recognized as a kiss off.

Barth's voice intruded on his thoughts. "Lamont? Lamont? Are you listening to me?"

Cranston turned to face him. "Sorry. What were we talking about?"

Barth exhaled in exasperation. "Lamont, I have never meddled in your affairs. All this constant traveling around the world to remote places and such. And when you disappeared for all those years after the war, I didn't ask any questions."

Cranston shot him a sharp look. He tolerated Barth because he had to: because he was Lamont Cranston's uncle and because he was the police commissioner and useful as such, inept though he was. But he was sometimes a meddlesome fool who had to be controlled. Unlike the former commissioner, Ralph Weston, a social climber who was continually trying to curry favor with the wealthy Lamont Cranston and too fatuous to pose problems of a personal sort.

Barth's mouth was open, as if his words about the war and Cranston's unexplained disappearance had become lodged in his throat. Cranston released his hold, and Barth said, "In fact, I don't want to know anything about what happened to you over there. Or where you went, or what you did. To be perfectly blunt, Lamont, there's something unsettling about you that's always frightened . . . your aunt Rose."

Cranston stared at him. "Aunt Rose, huh, Uncle?"

Barth cleared his throat meaningfully. "But this business with Hadley Richardson is different. You have to understand that your life is bound up with the lives of your family. As sole trustee of the Cranston estate, which provides a monthly stipend to all your relatives, you have responsibilities, Lamont."

The Shadow's whispered laugh of evanescent mirth almost escaped him. "Including you, Uncle."

Barth's gesture of dismissal was not altogether convincing. "That's hardly the point. You're simply not qualified to select investments without knowledgeable counsel. That fly-by-night electronics company you just bought into, for example. What is it? IBT? IBS?"

"IBM. And it's not electronics, it's business machines."

"That stock will be worthless in six months. Believe me, Lamont, the world will never be run by machines."

"Call it a hunch."

Barth sighed in exasperation. "Lamont, what do you have against taking advice? Why do you even continue to make plans for dinner when you know that you're only going to arrive late because of 'accidents' on the bridge?"

"Police Commissioner Barth?"

One of the club's messenger boys was standing over the table, a silver tray in hand. Muttering to himself, Barth began to read the neatly folded proffered note. Thankful for the opportunity, Cranston pretended disinterest. His eyes returned to the woman, who had been seated across the room, facing him. The tennis pro had come over to her table to light her cigarette and was leaning over her now, conversing in low tones, one hand on the back of her chair. She laughed courteously at something he said, then patted his other hand, sending him on his way. Her left leg was crossed over her right, her foot tapping to the band's rendition of "Some Kind of Mystery," the very picture of urbane sophistication. Her shoes were moiré pumps, dyed to match the dress. Twice, in eyeing the room, she glanced Cranston's way, concealing the flirtation with strategic sips from her water glass. Just now she had the wine menu in hand.

"What's the matter, Uncle," he asked Barth. "Cops and robbers business slowing down? Or has one of your canaries escaped?"

Barth took a sip of water and shook his head. "Another sighting of that damned Shadow character."

Cranston set his martini down more forcefully than he meant to. "I thought you said The Shadow was just a rumor?"

Barth's blunt fingers flipped at the note. "He is a rumor. But all of a sudden Duke Rollins doesn't think so."

"A duke, huh?"

Barth's expression soured. "A mobster we've been after. Wanted for murdering a cop. Half an hour ago he walks right into the Eighth Precinct and confesses, babbling that The Shadow made him do it. The desk sergeant says Rollins looked like he'd been thrown through a window. Rollins swears he's going straight—if he doesn't get the chair."

Cranston smiled to himself. When a crook went straight, The Shadow sometimes became his friend.

"But this Shadow is really beginning to get under my skin. Tomorrow I'm going to appoint a special task force to investigate this guy. We're going to find out exactly who he is, and we're going to put a stop to his interfering with police business."

Cranston leaned out of the light of the small table lamp, back into shadow. He raised his left hand to his chin, aiming the ruby-red ring at Barth. "You're not going to appoint a task force," he said, in the deep voice of his truer self.

Barth's head twitched. "No, the hell with it," he said after a moment. "I'm not going to appoint a task force." He seemed conflicted, embarrassed to have uttered his earlier statements.

Cranston remained in shadow. "You're not going to pay any attention to these reports."

"Ignore them entirely," Barth said, ridiculing the idea.

"There is no Shadow."

Barth raised his eyes and rolled his tongue in his cheek. "There is no Shadow. He's some kind of myth. If there were," he laughed shortly, "I'd be Eleanor Roosevelt." He screwed his eyes shut and leaned forward, pinching the bridge of his nose. He looked questioningly at Cranston, who was back in the light. "Where was I?"

"You were about to tell me who *she* is," Cranston said, indicating the ingénue he had noted earlier.

Barth squinted and nodded knowingly. "That's Margo Lane. Her father's a scientist, doing work for the War Department. Research and development, I think. Why, what's your sudden interest in her?"

"Uncle Wainwright, have you had your eyes checked recently? She's lovely."

"Maybe. But you better keep away from that one, Lamont. She's the source of as many rumors as The Shadow. Some say she's from Chicago and from family money, on her mother's side. But I've heard just the opposite, that she grew up on the wrong side of the tracks. Or at least until her father made a name for himself. He apparently couldn't care less about money, one way or the other."

"Married?" Cranston asked.

"Twice—if you believe the stories, once to a stock broker named Stevenson, then to a black from New Orleans. What's more, the word is she's strange." He tapped his temple. "Up here."

"Really?" Cranston said, intrigued. "Exactly my type."

5 The Shadow Revealed

How many more times was it going to take before this guy got the message? Margo asked herself. All his high-handed talk about tennis and yachting, when what she wanted was a taste of something new and different, something with an element of adventure, even danger, in it. But she couldn't be angry at Chad for trying. He was all about tennis and yachts; they all were, his whole clique of well-heeled bachelor friends. So she smiled, laughed at his jokes, and thanked her lucky stars when he finally returned to his table.

She tapped her foot to the band, to the clarinet player's melodic solo. She was accustomed to the flirtations and advances, and well aware of how good she looked that night. The gown had been dying to be worn, and she had refused to allow her father's last-minute cancellation to ruin the evening. Wild horses couldn't have stopped her. But to have showed up alone at the Cobalt Club! Lucky for her the maître d' had even agreed to seat her.

With Chad gone, she reached for the menu. There, too, nothing but the same old dishes when she wanted something with flavor, with spice. She should have gone to Little Italy, she told herself, or better still, to Chinatown. Well, a glass of something would help. She snagged a white-gloved waiter, bearing an open bottle of wine.

"Would you bring me a glass of Mouton—"

"Rothschild, Nineteen Twenty-eight," he said, showing her the label of the bottle.

"Why, yes," she said, at once surprised and delighted.

"From the gentleman," the waiter continued, pouring for her to sample.

"Gentleman?"

"Lamont Cranston," a voice announced.

He was standing at the table, one hand to the cummerbund of his tux, the handsome man she'd been flirting with earlier. He gestured to the chair opposite hers.

"May I?"

Encouraged by his choice of wines, she smiled, allowing a hint of suspicion. He was tall and impeccably dressed, but he spoke in a mannered way that didn't quite match the hard aspect of his face, which—while calm and well molded—was somewhat masklike, as if it veiled what lay beneath it. She was reminded of a man she met a year earlier, on a cruise of the Caribbean. He positioned the chair directly to her right, but before he could say anything, Chad was back, leaning between the two of them.

"One thing I neglected to mention, Margo. Some of us are going over to Billy Reed's place a little later on, and I was wondering if you'd join us."

"Chad," she said, "this is Mr. Cranston."

He looked over his shoulder at the man he was practically elbowing in the face. "Sorry to cut in like this, old chap, but it simply can't wait."

Cranston smiled without showing his teeth and touched his fingertips to his chin.

"Well, here's the thing," Chad went on. "You'll hear some great jazz, and it'll give us a chance to talk and get better acquainted. Or are you more the jive and boogie-woogie type?"

For reasons unexplained, Chad had picked up the bottle of wine and was holding it at waist level. Margo watched him, hardly hearing a word of what he was saying.

"We never seem to be able to hook up, you and I, and I—"

Chad had tipped the bottle to his cummerbund and was suddenly pouring the wine down the inside of his trousers. Margo's hand flew to her mouth, but not fast enough to stifle a laugh. "Chad, what are you doing?"

He looked down, then up at her in alarmed confusion. "Oh, my god," he sputtered. "Excuse me, excuse me."

He hurried away, leaving Margo to stare at Cranston in disbelief.

"People," he said, with exaggerated nonchalance. "It's interesting to note, however, that all three of us seem to favor the Twenty-eight."

Margo laughed out loud.

Cranston had a silver dollar in his hand, and was rolling it across his knuckles and making it disappear into his palm. "You know, it's the strangest thing," he said suddenly. "I have an irresistible craving for Peking duck."

The comment unnerved her. "That's so odd," she managed. "I was thinking earlier about Chinese food."

"Imagine the coincidence." His grin was roguish. "But, listen, since we're both craving the same thing, perhaps you'd join me for dinner?"

He stood up and offered her his arm.

Which she impetuously accepted.

* * *

"That was Chinese, wasn't it?" Margo asked after Cranston finished ordering and the waiter had hurried off to the kitchen.

"Mandarin, actually," he told her in false modesty.

Margo eyed him dubiously. "Is that right." She gestured with her chin to an Asian couple seated nearby, who couldn't seem to keep their hands off each other and were whispering intimately. "What are those two saying?"

Cranston smiled. "A test, is that the idea?" When she nodded, he leaned slightly in the direction of the couple and listened for a moment, his grin widening.

The decor of the restaurant was understated: Chinese silk screens on the walls, candlesticks and black enamel vases with sprigs of dried flowers on the tables. The tablecloths were salmon-colored and matched the window valences, and the china was emblazoned with hand-painted Oriental dragons.

"They'd like to sneak away for the weekend, but they're undecided on the excuse he should give his wife."

He studied Margo while she studied the couple. She was more petite than she looked from a distance. She had prominent cheekbones and her big blue eyes were widely spaced. Her nails were short and lacquered red, and her scent was Hermes No. 1. Her wavy hair was swept behind her left ear, revealing a dangling pearl teardrop. Rhinestone cuffs adorned both her wrists; a diamond-cluster cocktail ring, her right hand.

Margo forced an exhale. "Well, whatever he's saying, I wouldn't trust a word of it. He already has guilt written all over him."

Cranston's brows arched. "Does he? I hadn't noticed. But tell me, what exactly does guilt look like? Can you read it on a face?"

"I can certainly read it on yours." Margo's eyes went from Cranston's to the table.

He followed her gaze to where his hand rested atop hers. But instead of shrugging it off, she took hold of it, turning it over to study the palm.

"A very peculiar life line," she announced after a moment. "It splits in two, see?"

Cranston peered at the uppermost, slopping crease in his palm, which did indeed bifurcate.

"That usually suggests secrets, or at least a secret life. Do you have guilty secrets, Mr. Cranston?"

He acted unfazed. "One or two, perhaps. But doesn't everyone? Don't you?"

She laughed lightly—evasively. "None that are very exciting, I'm afraid. You, on the other hand—"

"So to speak."

Her smile tightened. "You strike me as someone with a dark past." When he didn't respond, she continued. "There's your affiliation with certain political groups, for example, and your reputation with women. . . ."

"Greatly exaggerated. It's just that I'm very sociable."

"Is that what we're calling it now—'sociability'?"

He rested his chin in his hand and gazed at her. "You have something against being sociable, Miss Lane?"

"Not necessarily."

"I'd love for us to be sociable together." His eyes probed.

"I'll just bet you would," she said knowingly. Then her hand went to her head, as if pained.

"Is something the matter," he asked in mild alarm.

She shook her head. "A headache, but different. It feels like—"

"Static?"

She glanced at him. The shadow of a passing waiter fell across her face. "Yes. But why would you say that?"

Cranston broke eye contact, suddenly angry with himself for toying with her. He hadn't figured her for the sensitive type, but she was, and she'd somehow sensed his gentle invasion of her thoughts. All to uphold his reputation as womanizer and thoughtless rake, a part he sometimes despised having to play, even if those manipulations did nurture his cruel streak.

"You're a very unusual man, Mr. Cranston," Margo was saying. "You knew my favorite wine, you guessed that I'd be in the mood for Peking duck. Now you seem to know what it feels like to be inside my head." She paused. "Not to mention that you speak *Mandarin*."

Cranston made light of it. "Perhaps it's just that we're compatible—sociably, of course."

She considered it. "Possibly. But I feel as though you're manipulating me."

"Why would I do that?"

"I suspect that you're trying to seduce me."

"You think so?"

"Call it a sixth sense. And while I suppose I should be flattered, I'm not entirely sure I trust you."

Cranston reached for the wine bottle. "More wine?"

The smile she returned was ambiguous. "You tell me."

Her apartment was in a brownstone on East Forty-second Street, number 67, on a tree-lined block with low hedges separating one staircase and stoop from the next. Shrevnitz drove them. Cranston held the door for her, then followed her to the foot of the granite stairs. The street and sidewalk were puddled with rain.

"Thank you. I had a wonderful time," Margo told him.

She wore a white, long-haired fox stole, with an elaborately beaded lining. It was tucked up under her chin and draped over her shoulders in a way that kept winter from touching her.

"I can't recall a more stimulating evening," he said, in the same counterfeit tone.

Dinner had gone smoothly if quietly. He had spent the time in his mind rather than hers. But the fact that she had responded to his earlier tricks was intriguing. In Tibet, he'd met adepts who could receive but not send; others who could only send; and still others with the ability to cloud the most balanced of minds. But because of her perhaps innate telepathic ability, Margo Lane was a potential threat to him.

"We should do it again sometime," she said now.

Cranston took too long to respond. "By all means. Let's."

Their handshake was nothing more than polite. But when he turned to head for the cab, something brought him back around. Margo, too, had turned on the stairs and was staring at him. Quickly, they covered the distance between them and slipped into each other's arms, kissing deeply, despite all that had been said, all that he'd been telling himself. But he wasn't alone in feeling bewildered. The kiss left Margo as breathless as it did him.

"Good night, Mr. Cranston."

"Good night, Miss Lane," he said, climbing into the Cord's backseat.

Shrevnitz let out a low, appreciative whistle while he was shifting from first to second gear. "I like her, boss. She seems different than most dames."

Cranston had his head angled to the rear window. Margo was still on the steps, gazing at the cab. "More than even she knows."

All the cavalier nonchalance had left his voice.

Shrevnitz cut his eyes to the rearview mirror. "I don't get it."

"I think she's completely unaware of her abilities."

"No kidding. That mean you're gonna see her again?"

"No, it's much too dangerous."

"Dangerous for who?"

"For me, Shrevvy."

The Cranston manse was only a few blocks north, on East Fifty-third, in Manhattan's Turtle Bay section. The huge house had a touch of French *pierre de taille* and was set back from the street by a semicircle of driveway that coursed through tall wrought-iron gates embellished with the letter *C* on a blue background. The Cranston fortune had been made in railroads and manufacturing, among other things, and had survived Black Friday by dint of the late Theodore Cranston's uncanny knack for the market. Cranston was one of few New Yorkers who hadn't sold his property to a developer because of the servant problem, or the escalating costs of maintaining fifty rooms in the heart of a thriving city.

The interior was lavishly appointed with brocaded drapes and couches, massive examples of hardwood furniture, and family heirlooms handed down by several generations of Cranstons. One entire wing had been given over to the treasures and trophy heads of game animals Lamont Cranston had collected in a decade of traveling to remote corners of the world. The house had the look and feel of permanence, as if the Cranstons were only the latest in a long and continuing line of distinguished occupants.

The man who had been masquerading as Lamont Cranston on and off for the past ten years was asleep in a crushed-velvet chair in the mansion's principal drawing room. An embroidered pillow rested in his lap, and in his dangling right hand was cradled a fluted crystal snifter. Only a small amount of brandy remained in the glass. Cranston's bow tie was loosened, and his tuxedo jacket was tossed over a nearby setee. A fire blazed in the marble fireplace, which was flanked by large urns containing long, feathery grasses snatched from some marshy environment. While he slept, a butler made a quiet entrance to fetch an empty plate from the table next to the chair and left just as quietly.

The real name of the man who had appropriated Lamont Cranston's life and was the black-clad crime-fighter the press had named The Shadow was Kent Allard.

Allard had been an aviator during the Great War, the war to end all wars, and it was in Europe that he first encountered Cranston, a man he so resembled that the two were constantly being mistaken for each other. Cranston was everything Allard wasn't: privileged, pampered, opportunistic. Allard had been horrified by the savagery of trench warfare and aerial combat; more so by his own barbaric fascination for violence and mayhem, a fascination that had been with him for as long as he could remember.

The sanctioned violence of the war had been meant to exorcise his bloodlust, but instead it had only loosed the beast within him. He grew more and more skillful at the art of war, and when deprived of it he had nowhere to turn but to the equally savage world of drug running. In Istanbul there had been another encounter with Lamont Cranston, who was himself involved in smuggling. Then an offer to partake of the opium trade had sent him to Asia and landed him ultimately in Tibet, where his fields had supplied markets in China, Europe, and South America, and where his experiences during the war had enabled him to vanquish any would-be rivals in the trade.

By then he was using the name Lamont Cranston, in the belief that his and Cranston's paths would never again cross. As for ace aviator Kent Allard, he was believed to have died in the subtropical jungles of the southern Yucatán Peninsula, during a reconnaissance flight over a newly discovered Mayan ruin.

It was only after his abduction and forced apprenticeship with Marpa Tulku that the faux-Cranston returned to the United States, changed for the good, redeemed, or so it seemed; fated to assume the form of The Shadow in his new mission to lay waste to crime. Aware that the real Cranston—celebrated explorer, big-game hunter, Industrialist and man-about-town—was frequently out of the country, Allard made use of their resemblance to insinuate himself into social circles that ordinarily would have been closed to him, hobnobbing with financiers and politicians, with police commissioners and dealers in rare art. Allard had sometimes worn other guises as well; that of Henry Arnaud, to name but one.

But there occurred an incident several years earlier that had since allowed Allard to go on being Cranston without fear of exposure. The real Lamont Cranston had returned from a trip to South America to discover that people were claiming to have run into him, at the Cobalt Club and elsewhere, even though he had been deep in the forested heart of Amazonia at the time. Alone in his bedroom in the mansion one night, and beginning to doubt his sanity, Cranston—no stranger to dark secrets—had been visited by his frequent impostor, The Shadow, and the mystery had been solved. Cranston had been so horrified by The Shadow's explanation that he had immediately agreed to go on lending his identity, as much to distance himself from the maniacal Kent Allard as anything else.

From that night on, for all intents and purposes, Cranston, Allard, and The Shadow were the same person.

The New York City manse was only one of Cranston's haunts; there were also the New Jersey estate—not far from Rahway; the Caribbean island facility, run by the criminologist, Slade Farrow; and a second place in New York, in a downtown apartment building, the rooftop of which was occasionally used as a landing pad for The Shadow's autogiro. A combination of Allard and Cranston money funded The Shadow's ongoing research into the deviant workings of the criminal mind, in addition to financing the implementation of the most up-to-date investigative techniques: the purchasing of information; the subsidizing of informants; the use of cipher codes; and the designing and installing of a byzantine communication system that allowed The Shadow to remain in close contact with his legion of field agents.

Just now, however, it wasn't Lamont Cranston who was dreaming but Allard himself, his eyes shifting wildly under closed lids.

Had the butler been a few minutes late in the performance of his duties, he would have been present to hear a low rumble fill the drawing room, to see the brandy snifter vibrate in sympathy, to watch the flames in the fireplace quicken and belch a swirling fireball into the room, swaying curtains and chandeliers, and to watch amazed as the brandy ignited, exploding the snifter. . . .

Cranston's eyes popped open, and he sat bolt upright in the chair. In what may have been no more than a vivid dream fashioned to safeguard his sleep, he had glimpsed the fireball, which should have torched the room, but instead had formed itself into a face of leering severity. A face born in the mysterious depths of Asia, that seemed capable of looking right through a person.

Then, as quickly as it had appeared, the face vanished, sucked back into the fireplace as if in reverse time-lapse motion, leaving Cranston to wonder at it.

Not since his dream in the palace on the night of his abduction had he experienced such raw, psychic power.

"Someone's coming," he heard himself whisper.

6 Exhibition of Evil

In its eagerness to drum up business, the New York Museum of Art and Antiquity, on Central Park West, was featuring two attention-grabbing exhibits: "The Dawn of Time" and "The Art of Flight," both advertised by bright banners festooned from the museum's ornate facade. A blockish five-story affair that sat directly on the street, the building's northeast and southeast corners were ornamented with towering, monolithic headpieces depicting the three Fates.

Inside, just now, Issac Newboldt, tenured curator of Asian sculpture and folk art, was scurrying through the museum's Hall of Dinosaurs—no match for the Natural History's collection, but well represented just the same. Newboldt was white-haired, sixty-two, tall and distinguished-looking, with a somewhat pointed nose and a grizzled mustache. His customary attire was a blue, three-piece suit and striped necktie. That he was still in the museum at eleven P.M. owed to paperwork that failed to diminish no matter how much effort he applied to it. And to make matters worse, Berger had phoned from receiving, requesting his immediate presence over some matter that had yet to be clarified. Newboldt checked his fobbed pocket watch as he hurried through the darkened display rooms and marble corridors.

Receiving was located on the ground floor in the rear of the building, just past the offices where staffers and aides tagged and catalogued items bound for display cases or the museum's vast, treasure-laden basement storerooms.

Pushing his way through double doors with pebbled glass panels, Newboldt entered a long and musty-smelling room, whose exterior brick wall was interrupted by three loading bays, sealed by roll-up doors. Off to one side of the room were a half-dozen full-size figures costumed in medieval Asian and European armor, and beyond them a squat, Egyptian mummy case. Elsewhere was a collection of grimacing wooden masks from Polynesia and the highlands of New Guinea. As ordered by Accounting, the lights were dimmed and, what with the dark corners and the murky shadows cast by the costumed figures, the place felt like a dungeon.

Berger was pacing anxiously in the center of a cement floor strew with packing straw and excelsior. At the receiving desk sat Nelson, an armed security guard, who frequently gave the impression of being afraid of his *own* shadow.

"What's so important that it couldn't have waited until morning?" Newboldt asked. His nasally voice reverberated in the room.

Berger gestured to an immense, slat-sided crate standing opposite the middle bay door. The crate was all of eight feet high and at least four feet wide and as many deep. Nested like an Easter egg in its packing, the rounded top of an elaborately carved coffin showed where a section of the crating had been removed.

"That's just it, sir," Berger said. "I don't know what it is. I'd have labeled it a mummy case, coming from Tibet, as it does, but—"

"A mummy case from Tibet," Newboldt said, in a patronizing tone. "Well, that's very interesting."

Berger nodded. A slightly built man with thinning hair, he wore a bow tie and wire-rim glasses. "Exactly what I thought. But this one seems to be metal. So I decided that it was more of a sarcophagus—"

"Oh, a *sarcophagus* from Tibet. That's a horse of a different color." Newboldt showed the younger man a disapproving look and took a step toward the crate. "Pay close attention, Mr. Berger, you're about to be educated."

Accustomed to the curator's condescension, Berger conjured an attentive look. Alongside him, with his mouth slightly ajar and his uniform cap crooked on his head, stood Nelson, small and baby faced.

"In Tibet, burial in the ground is reserved for criminals and people who die of contagious diseases," Newboldt began. "Beggars, widows, widowers, and the very poor are usually surrendered to rivers, as is done in the subcontinent. Tibet's scholar-monks are usually cremated, though Dalai and Panchen Lamas are often immured in stupas or chortens. For everyone else, the preferred method is celestial burial. The dead are wrapped in white cloth and kept for five days, then the body is transported to a high promontory, where it is hacked to pieces—bones and all—and fed to vultures. The birds are summoned by fires built from pine and cypress woods, and *tsampa*." Newboldt cut his eyes to Berger. "Now, what does our lesson suggest to you regarding this coffin or sarcophagus, as you say?"

"That it's probably not from Tibet?" Berger said sheepishly.

"Precisely." Newboldt glanced at Nelson. "Where are the men who delivered it?"

The guard shrugged. "Gone. They took off."

"Well, what does the shipping invoice state?"

Berger pulled the slip from his jacket pocket. "It says here that the shipment originated in Tibet. The delivery was made by the Integrity Transfer Company."

Newboldt snatched the invoice and read it for himself. "Obviously there's been a mistake. We're not expecting anything from Tibet—and certainly not some counterfeit sarcophagus. I'll have Acquisitions contact the customs broker to sort this out. In the meantime, let's just see what we have here."

Newboldt moved to the crate. The burnished surface of the coffin had an almost molten look, and the lid was actually made up of two full-length doors, hinged along both sides and secured where they met by five baroque latches, carved to suggest intertwined dragon's claws.

"Whatever its provenance," Newboldt commented, "it's exquisite." He ran a hand over one of the doors, then rapped his knuckles against it. "It's solid silver!" He turned to Nelson. "Give us a hand getting the sides off."

The crowbar Nelson had used to pry off the upper section of crating was still hanging from the lower portion, and Nelson used it to strip away the side slats and what remained of the front. Newboldt brushed the straw away and used his handkerchief to clean what looked to be a cartouche engraved into the right-hand door. Nelson appeared with the reading lamp from the desk.

"What's it say?" Berger asked.

"The writing is in Latin and what seems to be Arabic." Newboldt studied the letters intently for a moment. "No, I'm mistaken. It's in Latin and Uighur script."

Berger and Nelson traded ignorant looks.

"An alphabet borrowed from the Sogdians—an East Iranian people from Samarkand and Bukhara—" Newboldt stopped himself and inhaled sharply. " 'The Kha Khan,' " he said, deciphering the engraving. " 'The Great Ruler. The Power of Heaven, the One God, Tengri, on Earth. The Seal of the Emperor of Mankind, Ruler of All Tribes Living in Felt Tents.' " He looked at Berger and Nelson in undisguised astonishment. "Temüjin! This is the coffin of Temüjin!"

Berger had his mouth opened to respond when Newboldt continued.

"The man we've come to know as Genghis Khan—twelfth-century conqueror of half the world. Eldest son of Yesugei. Named after the slain tartar chief, Temüjin. The name approximates 'Smith.' The meaning of 'genghis' isn't known, but—"

Again, he glanced at the two men. "But this is impossible. Genghis Khan's burial site has never been found, much less his . . . his *coffin*. The body is thought to have been carried to Mongolia for burial on the sacred mountain, Burqan Qaldun, or perhaps along the upper reaches of the Onon. Forty women and forty horses were sacrificed, then the gravesite was trampled by hundreds of horses."

"So what's it mean, professor?" Nelson asked, breaking a brief silence.

Newboldt regarded him absently. "What's the address of the shipper?"

"The crate labeling only has the company name and the country of origin. No address for Integrity Transfer."

Plainly agitated, the curator checked his pocket watch. "I must make a phone call." He turned and started for the doors.

Berger looked at the coffin, then at Nelson, and said, "I'll, uh, help you, Mr. Newboldt."

"Nelson," Newboldt added, without bothering to turn around. "Whatever you do, don't open it!"

Right, Nelson thought as Newboldt and Berger were disappearing through the doors. Like I'd open the thing.

Favoring his right foot, he shuffled back to his desk and propped himself on the stool, turning his back to Genghis Khan's coffin. Glancing at a newspaper, he began to sing softly to himself.

"Come on along and listen to, the lullaby—"

A strange, clicking sound interrupted him, but he was unable to locate the source. Shrugging, he went on with his reading and his song. "The lullaby of—"

Again the sound interrupted him. But all at once it seemed to be coming from the vicinity of the coffin. Rats, he decided, a common enough freeloader in packing crates.

"The lullaby of Broadway—"

The sound returned, loud enough to startle him.

"Uh, Professor Newboldt, sir?" he called, in a weak voice.

When, after only ten seconds, Newboldt hadn't answered, Nelson slipped from the stool, drawing his revolver. The coffin's uppermost latch sprung open as he approached.

Holding the gun in one hand, he reached over his head and palmed the latch shut—only to see the lowermost of the five snap open. When he stooped to close that one, the top latch opened once more. And when he slammed his hand against that, the third undid itself, then the fourth, then the fifth, snapping open and closed, faster than he could attend to them, ultimately with such fury that the coffin started trembling and bucking.

Nelson backed away, his revolver raised, and gradually the latches' deafening tattoo subsided. But now he could hear a kind of thudding emanating from *inside* the coffin, and as he watched the unlatched doors parted, with a pneumatic hiss and an issue of what could have been smoke or a cloud produced by rapidly evaporating dry ice.

Inside the coffin, encased by moiré padding, stood the figure of a man. Powerful-looking though of medium height, the figure was panoplied head to foot in antique green silk that was studded with bronze disks and Chinese coins. It wore an elaborate, conical headpiece, whose quilted sides draped the figure's ears; a short cape emblazoned with flame and dragon motifs, and a black lacquer mask.

The figure raised its right hand and removed the mask, revealing a fierce, dark-complected Asian face, trimmed with a short, black beard. It inhaled deeply and let go of the mask, which shattered on the cement floor.

"I don't know how you got in there, buddy," Nelson managed, "but the museum's closed. N-next time, do like everybody else and pay your admission at the front door."

The Asian regarded him and stepped from the closet-size interior of the coffin. "Join me or die," he intoned in accented English.

"Say again?"

The man took another step in Nelson's direction. "Join me ... or *die*."

Nelson tried to avoid looking at the man's eyes but found himself transfixed, unable to turn his head, let alone to triggger the revolver. He swayed, holding the gun in front of him. "You're trespassing on private property."

The Asian showed him a look of utter contempt. "Your mind is *weak*. You aren't *worthy* of my presence."

Nelson swallowed and found his voice. "Don't come any ... any ..."

The Asian continued to close in on him, lifting his right hand and giving it a curious twist. "Fall to your knees and kowtow to me." Nelson dropped to his knees. Suddenly the Asian's hand assumed the profile of a gun. "Now, place the gun to your temple." The Asian's hand did that, forefinger for a barrel.

Horrified that his own hand was obeying, Nelson did as ordered, lifting the revolver to his head.

The Asian closed his eyes serenely and growled: "Now, sacrifice yourself to Shiwan Khan."

"Yes, my Khan," Nelson said with little hesitation, his trigger-finger free at last to execute his intent.

Newboldt and Berger were returning from one of the offices in the cataloguing section when they heard the report of the shot and quickened their pace to the receiving area. Newboldt had tried to contact his immediate superior but hadn't gotten through. Just as well, he had been telling himself. Naturally, the coffin would have to be authenticated. Then, too, there was the mystery of its late-night arrival—

"That's Nelson's gun!" Berger said.

Newboldt was second through the doors but the first to halt. Revolver in hand, Nelson was lying facedown in the middle of the cold floor, a pool of blood spreading around his head. Berger ran to him, winced, and shook his head at Newboldt. Newboldt turned away from the grisly scene and saw that the coffin was open.

And empty.

It was then that a disquieting feeling began to ladder through him. On first entering the room, he thought he had glimpsed an unrecognized figure standing amid the cluster of life-size statues of medieval warriors. His hackles up, Newboldt performed a cautious turn in the direction of the statues, but there were only the six of them he knew by heart.

7 Strange Bedfellows

With evil afoot, it was not a night for sleeping.

In room 2512 of the Federal Building, one in a copse of tall structures that comprised the heart of downtown, Dr. Reinhardt Lane was up late, tinkering with the device that had been his grail for the past decade. That the U.S. government had a strong say in what went on inside top-floor 2512 was evidenced by the two Marines who stood guard at the door to the laboratory, guns on their hips and hands clasped behind their backs. The door's glass panel read: WAR DEPARTMENT, RESEARCH AND DEVELOPMENT. REINHARDT LANE AND AUTHORIZED PERSONNEL ONLY.

Evil or no, it was Lane's habit to work early into the morning, amid tabletops cluttered with chemical glassware and technical instruments, wheeled chalkboards filled with esoteric scrawl, seemingly haphazard stacks of open textbooks and hastily scribbled jottings. Lane was in his mid-sixties, rangy, mustachioed, large-featured, and somewhat rumpled-looking in a brown wool tweed jacket with suede elbow patches and, that night, a finely striped, deep-red, cotton-flannel shirt. He wore oval wire-rim glasses and sometimes spoke with a slight brogue. The sort of hands-on scientist whose pockets were likely to hold an assortment of small tools.

Lane's wife had died years earlier, and his only child had moved into her own brownstone apartment. So why not work late, he frequently asked himself.

Lane was seated at his desk, bent over a soccerball-size orb of royal-blue alloy, into whose surface were secured some thirty or more relays that resembled spark plugs—the entire device held in place by a rig Lane had cobbled together using two plumber's helpers. Off to one side of the desk sat Lane's largely untouched dinner: a sandwich, an apple, and a bottle of Pepsi Cola. His mind was shut off from all distractions, including his chief distraction of the moment, Farley Claymore, colleague and reliable nuisance, who was hovering about, determined to make conversation.

"Didn't you hear me, Lane?" Claymore was saying. "I've completed work on the beryllium sphere. All that's left to do is run some submersion tests to verify the pressure calculations. I'm telling you, the army is going to eat this thing up."

Lane had a soft cloth in hand and was cleaning each plug before screwing it into the orb. He exhaled in irritation and swung to Farley. "Farley, our grant stipulates we're to engage in *energy* research, not weapons research. How many times do you have to be told that I'm not interested in discussing the potential military applications of our project?"

Claymore planted his hands on his hips and barked a laugh. "Don't kid yourself, Lane. This isn't Consolidated Edison we're working for, this is the *War* Department. They're not interested in 'viable' energy. And once they get their hands on that precious implosion orb of yours, you can bet your life they're going to find a military application for it. So all I'm saying is why not position ourselves to reap the financial benefits of our work by advising them of the potential?"

Lane was a physicist and chemist. Claymore's specialty was munitions, but he was also an engineer. He had a rectangular face, baggy though bulging eyes, a weak chin, and an unctuously ingratiating manner, well served by a mane of greasy black hair and a midnight-blue, single-breasted, wool serge suit with chalk stripes. The past five years had seen Lane and Claymore partnered on Lawrence's cyclotron project, Sherrington's research into subatomic particles, and Fermi's investigation of quantum states.

Claymore had lifted one of the plugs from their test tube–like rack and was fiddling with it. Lane wrenched it out of his hands and set to work cleaning it. "What the War Department does with the device is their business. I'm certain, however, that once they realize its potential for deriving useable energy from implosion that they'll do what's right. All that's required is a suitable fuel source."

Farley looked imploringly at the ceiling. "How naive you are, Doctor."

Lane bridled. "I would have gone to the private sector for funding if you hadn't convinced me that working for the government was the answer to our prayers. Who's to blame for that, Farley? Certainly not me."

A crazed grin split Claymore's face. "But the government could *be* the answer to our prayers if you'd only listen to reason. Your problem is that you don't think big enough. If you'd only let me handle things, the world could be our oyster."

Lane put his glasses on to examine one of the orb's threaded seatings. "Oysters give me a rash," he said, returning to his work.

"Ten-*hut*!" Farley barked, with a crisp salute for one of the Marines stationed in the corridor. The pair of them, in green woolens and white leggings, snapped to, straightening their shoulders and bringing their hands smartly to their sides.

Farley moved down the long corridor, a spring to his step, beaming in self-amusement. He wasn't halfway along when the elevator doors at the end of the hallway opened, revealing Margo Lane, wearing the same crisscross, cream satin gown she had worn to the Cobalt Club.

Farley sucked in his breath at the sight of her, practically gagging himself, and threw his arms wide as he hastened toward her. "Oooh, Margo . . . What a beautiful dress," he said, standing in her way. His eyes went straight to her cleavage, and he forced two short, lecherous exhales. "And s-such a *clever* neckline." He made that ga-ga sound again.

Margo smiled tightly. "Excuse me, Mr. Claymore, but I'd like to see my father."

She stepped around him and continued toward the office, but he wasn't long in catching up. He moved past her and leaned an arm against the wall, preventing her from passing.

"Uh, uh, Margo, authorized personnel only. But I suppose we can make an exception in your case." He was the would-be suave playboy now. "But first, tell me, when are you going to come down and see my beryllium sphere?" He cut his eyes to the dress, then showed her a dopey grin.

"I'm not interested in your ... spheres, Mr. Claymore."

Once more she stepped around him, and, undaunted, he pulled exactly the same move, playfully wagging his forefinger in front of her. "Margo, you don't return my calls anymore."

"That's not true," she said, leading him on before lowering the boom. "I never did return your calls."

Farley slumped in exaggerated defeat. "I know. And I can't imagine why."

Margo leaned toward him and lifted his chin, her touch enough to induce a moment of staccato panting. "Because I don't like you," she said in a slow, falsely intimate whisper that emphasized each word.

Farley's eyes were fastened to her bare back as she walked away; then he folded his arms across his chest and gurgled a laugh. "Fascinating woman!" he said, more to himself.

Margo made directly for her father's desk—which was never an easy task, what with the distillation experiments in progress on every countertop, the beakers full of bubbling liquids, the electrical current jumping between galvanic spheres. Lane, his tweed jacket hung on the back of the chair, was still leaning over his work, muttering to himself, oblivious to her entry. Quietly, she set her stole and beaded handbag down, moved around behind him, and kissed him on the cheek.

"Margo, what a nice surprise," he told her. "Have you had dinner yet?"

"Dad, it's two A.M."

He glanced absently at his pocket watch. "What are you doing up at this hour?"

"I couldn't sleep," she said evasively. Her gaze drifted to Lane's flannel shirt. "Dad, *where* you get this shirt?"

He studied it for a moment. "You said you liked me in green."

Margo nodded. "I do. But *that's* green," she said, pointing to his drinking mug. "This—" she pinched hold of the shirt "—is red."

"Green, red, what does it matter so long as the shirt's clean?"

She rolled her eyes and gave him another peck, then took the apple from his desk and walked the few feet to his cozy reading chair, settling into it with her legs crossed over the rounded arm.

"Dad, do you believe in telepathy? As a scientist, I mean."

Lane glanced at her while he worked on the orb with a small pair of pliers. "Mind reading?"

"Do you think it can exist between certain people?"

Lane stroked his chin. "Thoughts are not substantial things that can simply be passed along. We're talking about the electrical activity of the brain. Oh, perhaps with the aid of a device that could record those electrical impulses, then decipher and somehow transfer them. But between *people*—unassisted? No, I don't think it's possible. Though your mother certainly did. It was uncanny the way she sometimes knew what I was thinking. But I suspect that her gift was nothing more than a product of her powers of observation. No, I'm afraid I'd have to side with the Great Dunniger and say that telepathy is simply a case of stage magic."

Margo was fiddling with the stem of the apple and gazing contemplatively at the ceiling, where the banks of fluorescents, the city light through Venetian blinds, the humming arc lamps, and the Bunsen burner flames had conspired to create a dizzying chiaroscuro of flickering light and shadow. She reflected on her evening with the inscrutable Lamont Cranston, the chief cause of her insomnia.

"Somehow, I expected you to say that," she told her father at last. "But it's so strange. I've always had the feeling that there was this . . . indescribable connection out there, just waiting to happen to me. And tonight, suddenly, there it was."

Lane surfaced from a moment of intense preoccupation. "That's nice, dear. Although what you're saying suggests a belief in predestination—another scientific implausibility, unless we choose to posit the existence of faster-than-light particles to vouchsafe—" He caught himself running on and looked at her. "What exactly are we talking about?"

Margo's expression was wistful. "A man, Dad. And I'm probably never going to see him again." She took a bite of the apple.

"Why not?"

"It's just something I know. But while we were together I had the feeling that I could sense what he was feeling, and he could sense what I was feeling."

Was it telepathy, she wondered, or was her imagination getting away from her? Who had picked up whom in the Cobalt Club? And whose impulse had she been following when she hurried into his arms—his or her own? It was all too confusing. But she couldn't get Lamont Cranston out of her thoughts; he was there, haunting the space behind her closed eyes like some specter.

Margo heaved a dramatic sigh. "Now I'm completely and utterly depressed."

A calculation on one of the chalkboards had caught Lane's eye, and he was staring at it. "That's nice, dear," he remarked.

She looked over her shoulder at him and smiled to herself, recalling how frustrated her mother used to get with him.

The Hotel Monolith had been the talk of the town while it was being built. Designed by one of the city's finest architectural firms and financed by the city's most colorful developers, the twelve-story edifice had been called "an Industrial Moderne masterpiece" by critics. Plans called for an Egyptian Revival facade and lobby, with gilded columns, elaborate cornices, and balustraded balconies, and—contained within a cylindrical, rooftop rotunda—the Moonlight Café, whose dark blue ceiling was to feature an artificial moon among a starfield of tiny white bulbs.

But the hotel had never opened. Events took a tragic turn when the owner went bust in the Crash and later committed suicide. After languishing for two years, the Monolith was put up for sale and purchased by a wealthy Asian, who announced plans to complete it but had ended up razing it. One day the building was there, the next day it wasn't, almost as if it had vanished. Now the lot on which it had stood, on the northeast corner of Houston Street and Second Avenue, was filled with rubble and garbage that had yet to be removed, and encircled by a high, wire-mesh fence topped with strands of barbed wire. Though why anyone would wish to venture inside was anyone's guess.

Nicky Dano, a ferret-faced hackie in the employ of Bluebird Taxi, normally didn't question his fares about why they wanted to go to a particular place, but there was something about the bearded Chinaman who had waved him down fifteen minutes earlier, up near the Museum of Art and Antiquity. First off, what was the guy doing out on the streets at that hour of the morning? Then there was his getup—the shoulder-length, jet-black hair and the Oriental silk cape and skirt that made him look like he'd just stepped out of some Charlie Chan movie. All the way downtown, the guy'd been mum, but it was like his silence had filled up the whole cab. Nicky was glad to be giving him the air. Still, he couldn't resist asking.

"You sure it's one-*five*-eight Second Avenue you want, pal?"

The guy surveyed the vacant lot from the backseat. "That's correct."

"Suit yourself," Nicky said, shrugging and glancing at the meter. Because of the chill, he was wearing a brimmed cap and fingerless gloves. "That'll be four forty-five," he said, figuring a large tip for himself.

The man opened the driver's side door, as if he hadn't heard.

Nicky glanced at the rearview mirror. "What's the matter, Charlie, you don't parlay English? I said—" He met the man's gaze in the mirror and had a sudden change of heart. "I said, this one's on me . . . figuring the lateness of the hour and such." Then, by rote, he reached across the front seat for his clipboarded call sheet and began to jot down the address.

"What are you doing?" the Asian asked as he was about to exit the car.

Nicky didn't even look at him. "Just writin' down the drop-off address, angel."

"You mean to say that you're recording my destination?"

"Taxi commission rule and company policy."

The man fell silent. When he had climbed from the cab, he stood by the driver's window for a long moment, staring at something down the street. "Your auto needs fuel."

Nicky glanced at him. He knew that wasn't the case, but something made him check the fuel gauge. The gauge read close to full, but Nicky felt a sudden need to top it off just the same.

"Geez, I do need gas," he heard himself say. He wedged his pencil behind his left ear. "Thanks."

He wanted to ask the costumed Asian how he could have seen the gauge from all the way in the backseat, but he couldn't bring himself to do it. In any case, there was an open filling station not three blocks away, a truck from Johnsen Fuel conveniently backing up to the pumps.

Nicky grew increasingly eager to fill the tank. He revved the engine higher and higher until the motor was protesting and the cab was shuddering; then he dropped the car into gear with a crunch of gears and squealed down the street, passing by the vacant lot, heading straight for the fuel truck.

Nicky didn't see his former passenger's mouth twist into a strange smile, or hear the alarmed shouts of night owls walking near the filling station. He didn't feel the impact, either, or the searing heat of the ensuing explo-

sion, that threw the taxicab high into the air, inciner-
ating the station attendants, the driver of the fuel truck,
and a few of the bystanders.

Before fire engines had even been dispatched to the
scene, Nicky was dead, the call sheet that recorded
Shiwan Khan's destination curled and withering in the
flames.

There were times when the years of apprenticeship
he'd endured in Tibet weren't worth a plugged nickel.

He had dragged himself upstairs from the mansion
drawing room to the master bedroom, only to find that,
despite his best efforts, sleep refused to be courted that
night. The face in the fireball vexed him. And, too,
there was Margo Lane, stuck in his thoughts like a phonograph needle in the grove of a disk. His life had no
room for friends or lovers like Lane. His life as The
Shadow, that was.

Just now he was sitting in bed beneath a comforter,
his head resting against the headboard, a clothbound
book in his hands. He had on pajamas and a silk robe,
patterned in shades of brown and gold. The book was a
recent edition of *A Tale of Two Cities*. As to why he had
chosen that particular book from the library's hundreds
of volumes, he couldn't say.

Ten blocks to the south, Margo Lane, outside the
bedcovers in a peach-colored nightgown and a short-
sleeved, sheer chiffon robe trimmed at the hem in white
fox fur, also had an edition of the Dickens classic in
hand. It was close to four A.M. when she had returned
from her father's lab, but even then she couldn't sleep.

The bedroom was small and tidy. The wallpaper was
a busy fern motif, and above the bed hung two framed

prints of seashells. The night table supported a simple lamp with a fringed shade. Margo stopped reading long enough to take a cigarette from the case on the night table . . .

Just as Cranston was doing the same. He closed his gold case, setting it down on the nightstand's marble top, touched a gold lighter to the tip of the cigarette, and took a puff.

Margo exhaled smoke; then, vaguely dissatisfied . . .

Cranston stubbed out the cigarette in a glass ashtray. He returned his attention to the novel but soon gave up and tossed the book aside. The worst of times, yes, he could see that; but when was it ever the best of times? He reached for the light switch . . .

And Margo turned her light off.

But sleep continued to elude him. He tried facing left, then rolled over onto his right side, facing the expanse of empty bed.

As if to accommodate him, Margo shifted position, staring into the predawn darkness of the room.

"Someday," she whispered.

8 Agents of Influence

By sunrise the following morning the receiving entrance of the Museum of Art and Antiquity had become a crime scene. Three hours later the area was still cordoned off by a snarl of cars belonging to police officers, detectives, forensic specialists, reporters, and photographers, frustrating the efforts of truck drivers to deliver their loads, and of numerous assistant curators, anxious about those same deliveries.

Commissioner Barth had arrived at just past nine o'clock to lord over the activity. In and of itself, the apparent suicide of a security guard wasn't an event that would garner much attention from the tabloids. But this one—carried out in a museum, and under suspicious circumstances—was just the sort of lurid incident that could quickly become a front-page item in *The Classic* or *The Standard*. And Barth wanted to make certain that his name received frequent mention.

The triple-bayed receiving area was bustling when he entered. Cops in long black coats and shields were milling about, interviewing witnesses and picking over the straw-strewn floor in search of clues. While Barth watched, one of them draped a jacket over the corpse, whose bald head lay at the center of a small lake of coagulated blood. Police photographers wielding box cameras were snapping shots from every conceivable angle, and two medics wearing Red Cross armbands were standing by, waiting to carry the body out to the dead wagon.

Barth was dressed in a dark blue chesterfield and sporting a snappy fedora. Seeing him, a sergeant hurried over to give him the scoop.

The witnesses, Newboldt and Berger, had been thoroughly questioned, though in fact they hadn't actually seen Nelson trigger the .38 round that killed him. And while their story was consistent with the evidence, certain things didn't add up.

For starters, the casket, or coffin, or whatever it was. The shipper, the Integrity Transfer Company, didn't have a listed address in New York, or anywhere in Jersey or Connecticut. And yet the customs form indicated that the coffin had arrived in New York by ship, from Shanghai. The customs number on the shipping invoice matched that on the crate, which had been cleared through customs by someone who'd passed himself off as the curator of the museum. The crate had been opened for inspection, but the bogus curator had argued vehemently against opening the coffin itself, insisting that the 800-year-old mummy it contained would literally disintegrate if exposed to the air.

Nonetheless, the coffin had been opened, examined for contraband, and cleared. Interviewed over the phone, the inspector whose signature was on the form recalled clearing the coffin but claimed to have no recollection of examining the interior.

But where, in any event, where was the mummy? And why had Nelson—thought not to have been the bravest or brightest on the block—decided to open the thing?

Accepting for the moment that someone had concealed him or herself inside the coffin, the obvious question was: to what end? Alternatively, the coffin could have contained valuable contraband, which could have been hurried out of the receiving area during Newboldt and Berger's absence. Either way, poor Nelson might have been murdered, or even forced to shoot himself.

Powder burns on Nelson's right temple verified that the gun had been discharged at point-blank range, but you usually didn't find the heater in the suicide's hand, as had happened with Nelson.

Even so, there was little to support the murder angle: no signs of a struggle, no second set of prints on the .38, no evidence that anyone had entered the area through one of the bays, all of whose roll-away doors were padlocked *from the inside*.

So, until further evidence came to light, the detectives in charge of the case were forced to accept that Nelson had opened the coffin deliberately; then ... what? Croaked himself on realizing that he'd disobeyed Newboldt's instructions?

The curator himself had admitted to "sensing a presence" when he and Berger had reentered the area, though he hadn't been able to elaborate on just what that presence may have been.

As for the coffin, several museum experts were in agreement that it was certainly ancient and possibly genuine. However, as to whether it had once held the body of Genghis Khan, no one could say until the interior was tested for specimens of skin, hair, fabric, and whatever else. Since Genghis Khan's burial site had never been located—officially—some felt that the priceless silver coffin delivered to the museum may have been used to mislead any would-be grave robbers roaming Outer Mongolia in search of plunderable tombs.

The sergeant finally got around to apprising Barth that Detective Joseph Cardona had been placed in charge of the investigation.

The commissioner's only response was, "That one, huh? He's a joke."

In point of fact, Inspector Cardona, the only son of a veteran cop, was renowned for his investigative skills. Then assigned to the Twenty-sixth Precinct, he had been on the force for almost fifteen years and was rumored to wear his Police Positive in a custom-designed shoulder holster. Tall, muscular, and square-jawed, Cardona's well-known knack for blending effortlessly into any crowd or background rendered him a near perfect surveillance operative. If he could have been said to have a distinguishing characteristic, it would have to be the large, red-stoned ring he always wore on the third finger of his right hand. When people inquired about the ring, he fed them a story.

Cardona had observed Barth's arrival but was in no mood to talk to him. Given the many unanswered questions attending the security guard's apparent suicide and the suspicious delivery of the silver coffin, Barth was low down on Cardona's list of priorities. While the commissioner was being briefed, Cardona made an unnoticed exit from the receiving area and walked straight for his car.

He drove south along Broadway, then took Seventh

Avenue south to Twenty-third Street, in the heart of Chelsea—a district of warehouses, lofts, and import concerns—where he found a parking space in front of a tavern near the Lyric Theater. He then crossed the street to the Jos. R. Hunter Building, which he entered through the street-level offices of Lewis and Lewis, Chartered Accountants. Once inside the building, he continued down the first-floor hallway, past offices on both sides, until he reached a door whose pebbled glass panel said "B. Jonas" in black hand-painted letters.

Anyone peering through the grimy panel would have seen a darkened room, barren save for an overturned trash can. The doorway in one wall probably led to a closet.

Centered in the door's lower, wooden panel was a letter chute that had a hinged brass lid. Satisfied that he wasn't being observed, Cardona drew a creamy white envelope from the inner pocket of his coat. The envelope bore neither stamp nor address. He lifted the brass lid and bent to insert the envelope; it wasn't halfway in when it was eagerly accepted, with a quick but audible pneumatic hiss.

The letter chute opened on a pneumatic tube of the sort used to route mail through multilevel offices, or through entire buildings themselves. However, this particular tube—an open-ended, brass-banded canister waiting in its mouth—was part of a vastly more extensive network, years in the designing and installing, its existence known to a select few, its purpose not to undermine the U.S. mail system but to thwart the sinister spread of crime, as counterpart to the shady rumor mill of the underground.

The tube disappeared into the south wall of The Shadow's way station, where it made a ninety-degree turn and coursed through the chase wall of the building, sometimes running parallel to gas lines, pipes, electrical conduits, and air-exchange shafts, sometimes having the entire wall to itself.

It exited on the roof and plunged down over a ledge, around a corner, and up the side of an adjacent structure, before bridging a narrow canyon and penetrating the exterior wall of another building, where it cozied up to dumbwaiters and elevators, subflooring and lath, and wormed its way through the empty sash pockets of double-hung windows, winding and twisting its way through the hidden heart of Manhattan. . . .

Clattering along a brick wall over the heads of sleeping drunks and alley cats; masquerading as a radiator pipe bracketed to the kitchen ceiling of an apartment belonging to an elderly couple who dismissed the overhead rattling and the occasional chunk of loosened plaster for sympathetic subway vibrations; infiltrating an office, where the swift transport of its cargo set watercoolers bubbling . . . Through basements, up walls, across rooftops crowned with water towers, pigeon coops, toilet vents, and billboards, emerging finally at a distant egress elsewhere in the city, and discharging its canister into the waiting hands of the system's seldom seen postmaster, known to The Shadow's agents and operatives only as Burbank. A person as mysterious as the cloaked avenger himself, sole denizen of his hidden crypt, a creature who rarely ventured outdoors and who seemed to be as much a part of the system as the hardware itself: the pneumatic tubes, the canisters, the couplings and elbows, and the vacuum pumps that breathed life into them.

Was he forty years of age? Fifty? He might have been either. Did he sport a mustache or beard? He might have. Were his eyes blue, brown, green, some combination of all three? More than likely.

More than thirty pneumatic tubes spilled into his high-ceilinged room and curved down to enclose him on three sides, their gaping termini within easy reach. Seated in his swivel chair at his massive desk, he might have been master of some kind of perverse pipe organ. Four lights dangling from the ceiling cast a crazy quilt of shadows across the entire arrangement. A glass-blocked portion of ceiling revealed the rapid strides of pedestrians.

Affixed to one wall of the room was a large map of the city, overlaid with the silhouette of The Shadow and stippled with colored pins to denote locations whose import could only be guessed at. Crime scenes, surely. But what else: the residences and workplaces of agents? Of potential collaborators? Of the known enemies of justice?

Only Burbank knew.

On that desk sat a radio rig and its boxy microphone, a headset, a typewriter, a magnifying glass in a brass holder, books devoted to methods of encryption, pens of marbled Bakelite, message canisters, an extra pair of spectacles, an ashtray, a tall thermos filled with strong java, and a signet ring that stamped a profile of a shadowy figure in brimmed hat and cloak.

Cardona's envelope came into Burbank's hands—bony, manicured hands that disappeared into the gartered sleeves of a pin-striped shirt. Over the shirt he wore a brown tweed vest, whose matching jacket was neatly draped over the back of the swivel.

Burbank slit the envelope with an antique letter opener and studied the contents of the detective's short note. And even while he read, the hand that bore the ruby-red ring of fraternity was inching toward the inset button switch on the right side of the desktop.

Shrevnitz had had a slow morning, a couple of rides for the distance, an airport run, but most of the driving had been strictly round-the-block affairs. Bundled-up tourists, unwilling to walk from one trap to the next, not what you'd call your big tippers. Same was apparently true for his fellow hackies, most of whom were milling around in front of one sandwich joint or another, jawing about how bad business was instead of prowling for fares.

The middle-aged couple in the rear looked like a couple of out-of-towners, but they'd turned out to be from the Island, just in Manhattan to do some shopping. The guy was carrying two packages tied with twine; his wife's red hair came straight from a bottle, and she was wearing lapin and imitation pearls.

Shrevnitz had them figured for nickel tippers, so he was taking them a little out of the way, keeping them distracted—well, *entertained* was how he liked to think of it—with a nonstop monologue, one of his patented stories, maneuvering with the best of them, right arm flung over the seat back, corner of his left eye on the road.

"So I say to her, 'Shirl, what do we need a washing machine for, when we already got a washing machine. *You!*' "

The couple were clinging to each other like lint on velvet, terrified they were going to end their days in the back of a taxicab. The guy's mouth was half open, one hand pointing out the windshield.

"Uh, that car—that truck—that, that—"

Shrevnitz swung the Cord deftly around each obstacle—delivery truck, flivver, another hack—rescuing his fares from the brink without so much as facing forward. "So, you get it? I told her, *'You!'* " He laughed loud enough for the three of them.

It wasn't that he got some kind of screwy kick out of scaring them senseless. More like he just wanted them to return to their picket-fenced homes, in Westhampton or wherever, with interesting tales to tell about their exploits in the Big City. Top-flight Broadway shows, moving pictures, swank shops, crazy cabbies.

He was still laughing when the ring on his right hand began to glow. He swung around in the seat, bolt upright while he studied the pattern of the flashes. That much done, he threw the taxi into a sudden left-hand turn, cutting off a bicyclist and a Dodge pickup truck, and nearly running over a young kid in a brimmed cap.

He threw the Cord to the curb and whirled on the couple. "Out!" he told them.

The woman regarded him with blanched concern. "Here? But we're not anywhere near—"

"You're near enough," Shrevnitz cut her off. "Out."

The man led the way as they hurried to the sidewalk, indignant but relieved, scarcely getting the door shut before the Cord raced off.

"Maybe we should walk back to our hotel," the man said, clutching his chest.

"Yes, let's walk."

They hadn't gone a block when the kid in the cap bumped shoulders with the man, neatly lifting the guy's wallet.

Lamont Cranston had been dressing when his ring received Burbank's transmission. Much like Inspector Joe Cardona and so many others, Cranston had a story ready when people asked about the *girasole* ring—a fire opal, in whose strange depths ran an ever-shifting gamut of rainbow hues. Numerous stories, actually, though none ever touched on Kent Allard's short-lived career as a espionage agent known as the Dark Eagle in Paris, Berlin, and Moscow, his fling as a Royalist and supporter of Czar Nicholas, his brush with the Mad Monk Rasputin; or about the Sacred Cabochon of the subcontinent, which had spawned the myriad ovals The Shadow had dispensed over the years.

But unlike those scions, there was something hypnotic lurking in the iridescence of Cranston's stone, as if, in its lesser way, the ring had absorbed some of The Shadow's own mesmeric power.

Cranston was waiting at the front door of the mansion when Shrevnitz pulled up to the iron gate.

"Where to, boss?" the hackie asked as Cranston slid into the rear seat.

Cranston's response had an edge to it. "The Sanctum."

Shrevvy's big foot sent the gas pedal to the floor.

9 A Subterranean Summit

Shrevnitz jockeyed the hack through the traffic in Times Square. It was a bad time of day to be there—the matinees about to start, the soldiers on leave, the hawkers, three-card monte dealers, and pickpocket teams gearing up for action. And the traffic lights.

"I'm sorry, boss," Shrevnitz said. "There's no way to beat all these new lights they're putting up."

"Never mind," Cranston said from the rear, "I'll walk the rest of the way."

Shrevnitz angled the cab curbside, and Cranston climbed out. He put on his black homburg and set off at a brisk pace, one leather-gloved hand in the pocket of his overcoat as he negotiated the pedestrian flow. A couple of blocks away, he began to slow down, waiting for the crowds to thin out. Then, just past Zamansky Jewelers, he cut left into an alleyway, its brick walls painted with advertisements for Personality Cigars and Zalo bread. On the right was Stern Brothers, Embalming, then a local chapter of the Young Men's Total Assistance Society.

He walked under a rounded archway, past trash cans and wooden barrels, and made a right turn into what looked like an ordinary box canyon, whose rear wall was that of a low, brick building, with a couple of double-hung windows overlooking the alleyway. Drainage grates, just now blanketed with wet newspapers and autumn leaves, were set into the cobbled ground below the windows of what were seemingly basement apartments or storage rooms. A rusting fire-escape stairway climbed the right-hand wall of the canyon, and it was toward that that Cranston moved, not to ascend the flight but instead to place a hand on one of the steel stair brackets riveted to the outer face of the stringer. He accomplished this without so much as breaking stride, and continued on toward the back wall, where a curious transformation was already under way: the center portion of the grating had dropped to form three escalatorlike steps, and a door-size section of brick wall that contained one of the double-hung windows was sliding inward, just deeply enough to permit entry into the building itself.

Cranston took the stairs in stride and edged through the opening, making an immediate left-hand turn into a tight, dimly lighted corridor. Just inside the doorway on the left wall was an L-shaped metal bracket that was identical to the stair bracket. Cranston paused briefly to glance out the doorway, then slid the bracket toward him. With a hydraulic hiss, the two-foot-thick door reversed direction. In the dead end beyond the door, taking up several square yards, were the massive flywheels, pulleys, and chains of the mechanical apparatus that operated it.

The short corridor led to another set of iron stairways that right-angled down into an octagonal shaft, ten feet wide by some fifteen feet deep. No sooner did Cranston's black Oxfords touch the first landing than eight roll-up doors began to pocket themselves into rounded arches at the bottom of the shaft.

The doors opened on a larger octagonal space with exposed girder beams, out of which had been fashioned two contiguous rooms and a narrow corridor that angled around behind the stairwell. The walls were constructed of beige limestone, banded at intervals with blocks of a deep tan. Wall sconces and lamps bathed the rooms in a faintly blue light.

Cranston entered the sanctum's principal room and went directly to the desk, where he began flipping the toggle switches on a matte-black control panel. The desk encased him on three sides and was every bit as cluttered with books and devices as Burbank's. Its centerpiece, though, was a maple radio cabinet as large and curvaceous as a head-and-shoulders bust of Helen of Troy. Where the rig's tuning dial might have been was a silver disk surrounded by a spokelike array of slender light tubes.

The wall opposite the desk was a six-by-six-foot control panel, also matte-black, fed by electrical conduits three inches in diameter and surfaced top to bottom with coin-size red, green, and white telltales. Elsewhere in the room were Oriental rugs; a teletype machine; several Modernistic bronzes; a world globe as big around as a wrecking ball; and floor-to-ceiling cases crammed with books on criminology, the exact sciences, cryptography, the occult, law, anagrams, and stage magic.

Cranston sat in his black swivel chair while the sanctum's abundance of prototype electronic devices powered up; in a moment the radio rig's silver disk irised, and a noisy black-and-white image of Burbank appeared on a tiny circle of screen. Once, it would have been the image of The Shadow's agent, Claude Fellows, transmitting from the Grandview Building; but Fellows had been killed in action.

"Report," Cranston said into a microphone in a heavy stand.

"Our precinct agent reports a possible murder at the Museum of Art and Antiquity," a squinting Burbank answered him through the rig's speaker. "An elaborate coffin arrived from China during the night, and a museum guard is dead—made to look as if by his own hand. No suspects at present, but an investigation is in progress."

Cranston steepled his long fingers. "Murder," he mused.

"Agent suggests a separate inquiry may be warranted."

"Understood," Cranston said, keying the microphone's kill switch and returning some of the toggles to their off positions. He was just shrugging out of his overcoat when he perceived someone behind him whirl on the stairway.

Standing in the middle of the bottom flight was an Asian man, swathed in antique green silk patterned with dragons, his short cape embellished by a fringe of black goat fur.

"Somehow I pictured you as taller," the intruder said, affably enough. Compactly built, he had piercing eyes, shoulder-length hair, a thick growth of beard, and a crescent-shaped scar low on his right cheek.

"Who are you?" Cranston said, betraying little more than a hint of surprise.

"How unsociable of me. Shiwan Khan," he said, with a slight bow. "Most recent descendant of the Kha

Khans, Chingiz and Qubilai. You are, naturally, deeply honored."

Shiwan Khan continued down the stairs and stepped into the sanctum's secondary room. Content for the moment to allow Khan to reveal his purpose in infiltrating The Shadow's headquarters—no mean feat in itself—Cranston followed, laying his coat, hat, and gloves on a chaise longue. He had on a gray-checked Norfolk jacket with an action back, and a striped burgundy-and-white necktie.

"Under no circumstances feel obligated to introduce yourself," Khan went on. "I already know who you are." His eyes roamed over Cranston, and he made a gesture of dismissal. "Not this temporary version of yourself. I mean that I know who you really are—Ying Ko." He bowed his head, almost reverently. "I am a great admirer of yours."

The couch and an armchair in matching black leather sat on either side of a small fireplace, which was itself flanked by bookcases. On the wall above the mantel hung a impressionistic painting of a skyscraper. Near the couch was a mahogany sideboard, crowned with a Remington bust of George Armstrong Custer.

Cranston had adopted a casual pose by the chaise longue, one hand thrust into the pocket of his high-waisted trousers. The look he aimed back at Khan was innocuous. "I'm afraid somebody sold you a bill of goods, friend."

"Please," Khan said peevishly. "It is no more difficult for me to infiltrate your mind than it was this room." He motioned to the chair. "May I?"

Cranston gestured courteously.

"You disappoint me, Ying Ko. I would have thought

you'd enjoy meeting a kindred soul—someone else possessed of the ability to cloud the minds of inferiors."

Shiwan Khan employed the Tibetan phrase Marpa Tulku had used. "You were a student of the *tulku*," Cranston said after a moment, dropping all pretense.

"*Tulku?* What an honor you pay him. But yes, I was. Selected as you were—to be redeemed from a nefarious past. He spoke of you constantly, right to the last. But I'm afraid he wasn't able to turn me quite as easily as he did you." Khan paused. "You wouldn't happen to have any American bourbon, would you? I've developed a bit of a taste for it, you see." His right hand went to the sash of his silk tunic. "I'd be happy to pay."

Cranston went to the sideboard and took out two glasses and a bottle. "If I recall, your ancestors had a fondness for drink, among other things." He glanced over his shoulder at Khan before he poured the bourbon. "Do you want to talk about your visit to the Museum of Art and Antiquity last night?" He carried the glasses across the room, handing one to Khan, who stood to accept it.

"Wonderful collection of Tibetan tapestries."

They clinked glasses and sipped their drinks.

"Ah, Ying Ko," Khan said, "grown men still shiver at the mere mention of your name. Your raid on the village of Barga?—a master stroke. Swift, vicious, preemptive. I made a keen study of it. You are, I must confess, my idol." Khan appraised Cranston's expression, pleased to see a glimmer of pride. "Ah, so you remember it."

"It . . . rings a bell."

"A bell?" Khan said in exaggerated disbelief. "To be sure, a *Neban* bell from the Temple of the Cobras." He set the glass down on a pedestal that supported a Greco-Roman bronze, and walked into the control room.

Again, Cranston followed. "So tell me, what brings you to the Big Apple—aside from an elaborate coffin, I mean."

Khan smiled faintly. "Why, destiny, of course. Temüjin conquered half the known world in his lifetime. His descendant Qubilai Khan went on to conquer most of China, including Tibet. I intend to finish the job."

Cranston considered it. "Yes, but if I'm not mistaken, your ancestors were backed by armies of one hundred thousand Mongol horsemen and an infantry of Chinese bowmen. How do *you* plan to do it?"

Khan's ambiguous smile held. By now he had circled through the stairwell arches and was back in the sitting room. "If I told you, Ying Ko, it wouldn't be a surprise. But know this much: I traveled from Asia in the holy crypt of Kha Khan in order to absorb his power. In three days, on the day of the Chinese New Year and on the anniversary of his birth in the Year of the Swine, the entire world will hear my roar and willingly fall subject to the hidden empire of Shang-tu—what you in the West call Xanadu."

He paused for a moment, peering intently at Cranston. "That's a lovely tie, by the way. May I ask where you acquired it?"

Cranston fingered the Windsor knot. "Brooks Brothers."

"Is that Midtown?"

"Forty-fifth and Madison," Cranston said in a rush; then: "You—" gesturing with a forefinger "—are a barbarian."

"Thank you," Khan returned, sounding as if he meant it. "We both are." He closed on Cranston. "I know that inside you lies a lake of darkness. You dip into it every time you put on the hat and cloak of your alter ego. Veiling your mouth, encircling your ring finger, moving in anonymity ... Just as you were instructed to do to ward off possession by *evil*."

Without warning, he took hold of Cranston's wrist, holding on to him while he continued, hissing rapid words, low and urgent.

"Join me, Ying Ko, despoiler of Barga, butcher of Lhasa. You, and only you, deserve to rule by my side."

Cranston broke free, even while deliberately allowing himself to be backed against the wall where the sitting room and control room met.

"Together, we'll pit armies against one another, as in a game of chess," Khan was saying. "We'll collect our due of pain; we'll bathe our hands in blood. Your mouth still waters at the prospect of *real* power. I'm offering you a chance to recapture your past. Become my partner, Ying Ko!"

Cranston's back was to the wall now. "I don't answer to that name any longer."

"What's in a name, *Lamont Cranston*?" Khan motioned broadly to the control room. "Would you deny that this, all this, your entire mechanism for fighting crime, was financed by opium? Would you deny that you had a hand in creating the addiction for heroin that has settled as a plague on your precious America?"

In one rapid motion, Cranston kicked an area of the block wall at knee level, exposing a secret compartment whose door was hinged along the bottom edge. Reaching down, his left hand took hold of a nickel-plated, nacre-handled automatic—his never-before-flourished ace in the hole for just such an occasion.

But Khan seemed to have second-guessed him. He was standing by one of the shaft's arches, his hand at the sash of his tunic. "For the bourbon," he said, flinging something in Cranston's direction.

Reflexively, Cranston's right hand caught the object in midflight. And in the same moment, Shiwan Khan was gone.

"We'll speak again, Ying Ko," came a distant voice, seconds before the sound of the clockwork door mechanism rumbled through the room.

Cranston glanced down at the object in his hand—a coin of dull, yellow metal with a square hole in the center, larger than a silver dollar and engraved with what might have been Uighur script.

Shiwan Khan had spared no expense in appointing his throne room, a spacious surround of elegance, one-hundred feet in diameter, whose soaring ceiling was supported by a ring of columns as thick as oaks. The columns stood on plush, deep-blue carpeting, and their capitals met the ceiling in rainbow starbursts. Decorated with spirals and mandalalike mosaics, the central area of the floor was a sunken circle, four broad steps below the columned ring.

The throne itself was wide and high-backed and had two slender arms. Facing south, it sat beneath a half-circle canopy meant to symbolize Tengri, the One God, the Eternal Heaven, who was worshipped at the tops of sacred mountains in Mongolia. On either side of the throne stood gilded torchieres that resembled papyrus columns, and behind it was a tapestry that had hung in the court of the Kha Khan. On tables rested other priceless objects transported from Mongolia and Sinkiang: golden effigies, ritual knives, and the *Altan Debter*, the Golden Book, in which was written—in Chinese characters to represent Mongolian phonetics—the most secret history of the Mongols.

The room had been financed by liquidating a small portion of Khan's treasure trove, which included what had been bequeathed to him by his ancestors and what he had acquired on his own in half a lifetime of evildoing.

With Shiwan Khan were the twelve members of his inner guard, Mongols whose faces were high-cheekboned and more dark-complected and round-eyed than the Chinese of other provinces.

Genghis's guard had clothed themselves in fur hats with earflaps, felt boots, and fur coats that reached below the knee; in battle they had worn metal helmets and armor made from strips of strong but supple buffalo leather, several layers thick. But different times and different climes called for different uniforms.

Shiwan Khan's dozen wore tunics of patterned maroon silk with embroidered hems, baggy silk trousers, and knee-high black boots. The sleeves of the tunics covered their hands in a simulation of hooves, for—lessers of the Khan—they were nothing more than beasts of burden. Their breast and biceps plates were shingled with hundreds of ancient coins and two-inch-long rectangles of sharpened metal, and over their middles they wore a hubcap-size shield. Some carried folding crossbows over their shoulders—the *nou* of old; others, long, curving sabres that dangled from their red waist sashes.

Many a bribe had been paid, many a string pulled to get them into the United States, but what was influence if it couldn't be peddled.

Just now, the guards were lined up in two rows in front of the throne, and Khan was stepping down to review them, evaluating each as he meandered. Then, satisfied, he positioned himself at the foot of his throne and addressed them.

"The day of the Mongol warrior is once again at hand."

Acquainted with the litany, the dozen responded with loud hissing sounds that increased in frequency and volume as their emperor continued.

"Soon, with wings outstretched—" he lifted his arms in a dramatic gesture "—we fly to our destiny!"

Those with swords drew them from their scabbards in salute, arranging their glinting weapons in such a way that they formed the Chinese character of conquest!

10 A Deadly Contest

"**G**ood Morning, Mr. and Mrs. America and all the ships at sea!" the newscaster's voice blared from the bread-box-size radio in the Tam kitchen. "Flash! New York City reels from yet another reported sighting of the elusive creature known as 'The Shadow,' object of police, press, and perhaps most of all, racketeer interest for almost five years now."

Dr. Roy Tam looked up from the morning edition of *The Classic* to give the radio his full attention. He was seated at the head of the table, the kids to either side of him, working on homework they had postponed from the previous night.

"This most recent sighting took place on the Harlem River Bridge and comes to us courtesy of none other than one of the city's most notorious hoodlums, Henry 'Duke' Rollins, who turned himself over to police custody after what must have been a soul-searching encounter with The Shadow."

Tam's apartment was a modest street-level affair at 359 P Street in Queens, though Tam was proud of the new two-hundred-dollar GE refrigerator that took up an entire corner of the kitchen. Mrs. Tam, a slender woman with lustrous black hair, stood by the sink preparing box lunches for the kids. The room's window was almost directly under the granite staircase to the first-floor apartments, but just now it was admitting an oblique ray of sunlight.

"New York City remains divided as to who and what The Shadow is, and on just what side of the fence he sits. Is he the foe of mobbies, sharpsters, grifters, charlatans, and the rest of the city's riffraff? Or is he simply one of them, nursing a dream of becoming a big boss himself? What do you think, radio land—friend or foe? Where do *you* stand?"

Roy Tam swallowed hard, thinking back to the night on the bridge.

"My teacher says they just made up The Shadow so we'd listen to the radio more," Tam's youngest commented, looking up from his schoolwork. "Is that true, Dad?"

Tam looked at him. "No, it's not—that is, I'm sure that your teacher—well, I mean, it's possible, of course. Not that I would have any personal knowledge, one way or another. . . ." He allowed his voice to trail off and cut his eyes to his wife, who was eyeing him curiously.

"Is anything the matter?" she asked.

Tam had his mouth open to respond when a knock at the front door brought him to his feet. "I'll see who it is," he said, covering for his overreaction.

Trembling when he reached the hallway, he took a few calming breaths before opening the door a crack. There, in the sunken court, stood a tall, broadshouldered man, wearing a black homburg and an expensive, black wool overcoat.

"Yes?" Tam said, not quite sure if he should open the door any further.

The man held up his left hand to display a ruby-red oval. "The sun is shining," he said.

Tam gulped but managed to summon the correct response. "But the ice is slippery." So much for waiting a lifetime to speak those words, he told himself. Scarcely thirty-six hours had elapsed since he'd been recruited.

The man nodded, and Tam stepped outside, pulling the door halfway closed behind him. "You're an agent of The Shadow?" he asked in a conspiratorial whisper.

The man scowled. "Who?"

Tam showed him a blank look, then said, "Oh, yeah, right." He winked. "Gotcha." His initial nervousness was beginning to wane; after all, there was something exciting about being in on a secret the size of *The Shadow*. "What do you need?"

"A metal analysis—" the man told him "—of this." The way a magician might, he conjured what looked like a large coin from the palm of his hand.

Tam's laboratory was in the basement. A wooden stairway led down into a fifteen-by-twenty-foot room whose every horizontal surface was packed with the tools of his trade: racks of glass-stoppered bottles of agents and reagents, mortars and pestles, hydrometers and vacuum jars, graduated cylinders, beam balances, the usual hodgepodge of books and cryptic jottings. But of all that, Cranston's eye was initially drawn to the flyswatter hanging on the wall.

Tam had gone right to work on analyzing the coin. It was clear that the metallurgist had his suspicions about its composition, but he had thus far kept those to himself. Just now the coin lay in a petri dish, in an alkaline solution, to which Tam was adding drops of another solution, muttering to himself that he might have to conduct a spectrum analysis of the results. Cranston was standing alongside him, his coat over one arm.

Tam hadn't added four drops to the base when the liquid in the glass dish began to fizzle and grow dangerously agitated. Seconds later the dish shattered, and the metallurgist leapt back from the countertop in a mix of awe and dismay.

"It's simply too fantastic," he said, more to himself.

What was fantastic to Tam was probably going to end up a peril to everyone else, Cranston thought.

The Shadow's agents had begun to run backgrounds on Shiwan Khan, and a few facts had already come to light. Using various front companies, Khan had been procuring arms and munitions and shipping them to his headquarters in Sinkiang Province in western China. Sinkiang lay between the Tibetan Plateau and the Gobi Desert of Mongolia—between the lands where mind and brute strength respectively reigned. Whether Shang-Tu—Xanadu—was an actual place or a product of a madman's imagination had yet to be ascertained. But Khan's goal of global domination was something that had to be taken seriously.

Cranston's own research had revealed that the notorious progenitor of the Khan line had been a man of unusual self-control. After succeeding to a position of command, Genghis Khan never again rode at the front of his troops, and was seldom far from his imperial guard of archers and swordsmen. A network of riders, known as the *yam*, kept him apprised of news in conquered lands. He hadn't so much developed new techniques of warfare as perfected the methods of his predecessors. It was from the Chinese, for example, that he had learned the use of siege machines, like catapults, battering rams, kedges, and naphtha-barrel throwers. More, he was obsessed with immorality and had spent a good part of his life in search of the alchemical "philosopher's stone."

"Bronzium," Tam was saying, marveling at the dull yellow coin. "That's what the ancient Chinese called it, at any rate. They believed it to be the very stuff from which the universe was formed." He looked hard at Cranston. "How did you come by this?"

Cranston stroked his chin. He had first taken the coin for a talisman or a ritual object of the sort that was left on the tongues of the dead to assure entrance to the Mongol's version of heaven. "I believe it was brought here from Sinkiang or Mongolia," he told Tam.

Tam nodded. He had the coin in the grip of tweezers and was hurrying it over to a microscope. "That would certainly be consistent with the legends about bronzium. Sinkiang was considered to be the navel of the world."

"Could bronzium be used as an explosive?"

Tam was hunkered over the scope's eyepiece. "Theoretically. You see, it's a naturally occurring isotope of uranium, extremely unstable at the atomic level." He straightened in what seemed like sudden realization. "In fact, we've probably dosed ourselves some by handling it." He got up from the stool and went to consult a textbook, flipping through the pages while he spoke. "The isotopes's explosive potential can be released only by dividing the mass into separate parts and then bringing those parts into contact once more, resulting in a kind of nuclear fission."

"Could the explosive potential be released by a charge of dynamite or nitroglycerin?"

Tam returned to the stool with the book in hand. "Not according to the latest research. Those who've been experimenting with fission suggest that the effect could only be achieved by *implosion*—an inwardly directed burst of raw power."

"Just how powerful would the resulting explosion be?"

Tam gave his head an ominous shake. "No one can say." He went to one of the lab's chalkboards, cleaned an area with an eraser, and began chalking calculations. "Once implosion was achieved, the breakdown would spread rapidly to all levels of the atomic structure. Fashioned into a implosive/explosive submolecular device, the destructive potential would be nothing less than catastrophic."

"An atom bomb," Cranston mused.

"Hey, that's catchy," Tam said. Then it was back to business. "But one would first need some sort of initiator, something to get the chain reaction going. The latest thinking is that beryllium could fit the bill. Bombarded with polonium, for example, beryllium readily surrenders neutrons, with very little of the gamma radiation one finds in bombardment by radium."

"The free neutrons would initiate bronzium's fission explosion," Cranston said.

Tam drew three concentric circles on the chalkboard and pointed to the innermost one. "You begin with the beryllium-polonium initiator. Around that you place your bronzium core, which you've packed inside an array of shaped charges to provide the necessary implosion. You contain the whole package in a shell—it could be beryllium as well, to enhance the blast potential—and there you have it: Your atom bomb."

Tam stopped to regard his drawing, then set the chalk down and snorted a laugh. "But we're dealing with theories, none of which have been proven. And we're talking about devices that haven't even been designed, let alone constructed and tested."

As a student of Marpa Tulku, Shiwan Khan had been taught the importance of constructing a sanctum. He was in that sanctum now, a small chamber off the throne room, whose entrance was concealed by golden curtains. But where the sanctum of the *tulku*'s pet student was filled with gadgetry, Shiwan Khan's was decidedly low technology: a small shrine to the Protector of Tents; a few candles, incense pots, brocaded pillows; a rug and meditation platform; and, on the wall, a Tibetan scroll—a *thangka*.

Atypical of the hand-painted, traditional depictions of Buddha, the scroll dominating the wall in the meditation chamber was a large rectangle of scarlet, emblazoned with an arabesque of interlocking geometries. Together, the overlapping circles and squares formed a bird's-eye view of an intricate maze of narrow passageways. Secondary colors and shading created an illusion of depth and movement, which forced the eyes to shift from one focal point to the next.

The *thangka* had belonged to Qubilai Khan, self-proclaimed Emperor of the Yuan Dynasty, who had ruled over China and Tibet, then known as Tubo. Shiwan Khan had acquired the tapestry from a *ngagspa*, a Bon sorcerer who had been assimilated into Tibet's official clergy. The sorcerer had worn an apron whose rigid superstructure was composed of human bones.

Prior to meditating, Khan always removed all jewelry

and drew the golden curtains, even if the throne room was unoccupied. Solitude and silence were important to concentration, especially when the goal was to send messages on the wind. It was essential that the adept enter a trance of one-pointedness and empty the mind of all cogitation.

Chiefly he had to free his mind from concerns about Ying Ko. Knowing Ying Ko, his reluctance to take part in Khan's plan was based on nothing more than wanting a full share rather than a fifty-fifty split of the world. But world domination was never easy. Chingez had faced his challenges; so had Qubilai. And so, too, would Shiwan Khan. It was all a game really, one he hoped he had set in motion by penetrating Ying Ko's *gentleman's* sanctum and leaving behind the coin. Was Ying Ko clever enough to pursue the lead? Time would tell. Meanwhile, phase two had to be initiated—piecing together the team that would make good on his promise to roar loud enough for all the world to hear.

Facing the *thangka*, he kneeled on the mediation platform and brought his ringless hands together in a resounding clap. Over his shoulders he wore a robe of black silk, trimmed with goat hair and heavy with gilded beading. The robe's patterns matched the floor, along which the garment spilled in a train four feet long.

He let go of all thought and fixed his eyes on the scroll's complex patterns, while his hands moved like those of a Balinese dancer, summoning the power. He pressed his fingertips to his shoulders, clapped once more, then touched his hands together before letting them resume their wavering dance in the chamber's incense-laden air.

The squares and circles seemed to lift from the *thangka*'s surface and embrace him in the maze. His dancer's hands pushed the power into his forehead, making him one with the labyrinth. He paused to cross his arms in front of his chest; then he began anew, fashioning a passageway for himself through the nonordinary world his mind had brought into being. And when he was confident that he had untethered himself from the physical laws that governed the mundane dimension, he flew through the city's forest of skyscraping towers to the man who was to become his servant in ushering in the cataclysm. . . .

Pencil in hand, Reinhardt Lane was working through supper again. But what was time but a construct—relative, ultimately inconsequential. On the desk sat the object that had come to tyrannize his life: the blue orb, whose descendants he hoped would provide clean energy for the world's hundreds of millions. But just now he was stumped and fatigued from the effort of rooting out errors in his calculations.

So fatigued, in fact, that he actually experienced an auditory hallucination of someone calling his name. So lucid was the voice that Lane actually turned to look behind him, certain that someone had entered the lab through the balcony doors. Not that unobserved entries were anything novel; just the previous night, Margo had made it all the way to the desk before he became aware of her.

Hearing the voice a second time was a clear signal that he needed a break. He set the pencil down and lifted his glasses onto his deeply creased forehead to massage his eyes with the heels of his large hands. De-

ciding that a breath of fresh air might be in order, he
got up and went to the balcony doors, covering the few
feet like a sleepwalker.

All four corner offices on the Federal Building's
twenty-fifth floor backed up to balconies. A ten-by-
twenty-foot space bordered on its outer edges by a low
retaining wall, the lab's balcony was representative of
the lot of them. Tubular light fixtures were bracketed to
the wall, and overhead was a shallow overhang that
formed the lip of the Federal's steeply pitched copper
roof.

Lane moved distractedly to the balcony's short wall,
at the outside corner of the building, and gazed down
on automobile traffic. It was only eight P.M., and the
streets were still busy. On the roof of the building
across the street was a billboard for Llama cigarettes—*a
blend of Peruvian and domestic tobaccos.* Llama was
spelled out in bold letters, with the phrase, "I'd climb a
mountain for a Llama," below it. And centered in the
advertisement was the face of a contented smoker, a
cigarette in hand, from whose rictus of a mouth issued
synthetic smoke rings at the rate of one every two seconds.

Lane regarded the billboard for a long moment; then
he reached into his trousers pocket for a smoke and lit
up, hardly taking his eyes from the sign. He had always
had it in mind to discover just what fueled that billowing machine. But all at once something else was
edging into his awareness. The smoker's face had begun
to shimmer and blur.

Lane averted his eyes and pinched the bridge of his
nose. But when next he looked, the face indeed seemed
to be reconfiguring into that of a long-haired Asiatic

man, with a crescent-shaped scar low on his right cheek and black eyes that transfixed.

"Reinhardt Lane," a voice in Lane's head intoned.

Lane regarded the sign mutely.

"Reinhardt Lane, you have been living a lie. You are not Reinhardt Lane at all, but Shan Juchi, from Sinkiang, a descendent of the vizier to the court of Chingez Khan, and presently the servant of the Kha Khan's inheritor, Shiwan. Do you understand, Shan Juchi?"

Lane's eyes had glazed over. His jaw was slackened and he swayed on his feet. "Yes, my Khan."

"That's good, Shan Juchi, because it is time to demonstrate your worthiness by using your creation to bolster Shiwan Khan's promise to unify the world."

Khan's frightening visage wasn't confined to the billboard any longer; it floated, large as a house, in front of Lane. "But the device isn't ready yet," Lane said.

"Then you can ready it in the presence of your master. Prepare the device for transport. An escort will be dispatched to assist you."

"I understand," Lane said, in the unsettling monotone of the hypnotized. "I will wait and go with them."

11 Steak Knives and Crossbows

Commissioner Barth was just finishing dinner in the Cobalt Club when Cranston slid into the chair opposite his.

"You know what puzzles me, Lamont?" Barth said, putting down his silverware. "How a man with absolutely nothing to do can be late for ever single engagement."

"Practice, Uncle Wainwright," Cranston said evenly.

Barth scowled and called to the waiter who delivered Cranston's martinis, "More sour cream!" Then, to Cranston: "I take it you've eaten."

Cranston stirred one of the martinis with his forefinger and tossed an olive into his mouth. "If olives count."

Barth had a rebuke ready when he spied Margo Lane standing in the Cobalt's winged archway. "It's that damn Lane woman again," he said under his breath.

Cranston swung around and saw Margo making a beeline for their table, dressed to kill in a green cut-velvet gown and a black fur. There was something angry in her stride.

"She's been phoning my office all day," Barth continued, just loud enough to be heard. "I practically had to resort to hiding under my—" Margo was on them suddenly, arms akimbo, and Barth segued into a cheery greeting. "Wonderful to see you again—"

She glowered at him. "You can drop the act, Commissioner. I want to know what you've done about my father."

Barth patted his downturned mouth with a napkin. "As I'm sure my secretary told you, Miss Lane, there *is* nothing we can do unless—"

"Unless what? He blows himself up?" For the first time, she looked at Cranston.

Barth caught the eye contact. "Miss Lane, I think you already know my nephew—"

"Yes, we've met," she said, forcing a smile.

Cranston stood up and motioned to the chair between his and Barth's. Barth shot him a sharp look that was too late in arriving. "Please," Cranston told Margo.

Margo sat down. The gown's scoop neck was black chiffon, shimmering with bugle beads and asymmetrically cut gunmetal. Her earrings were emerald-cut, and there was a square ring on the third finger of her left hand. Cranston leaned back in his chair to take her in.

"The fact that your father is behaving strangely is hardly justification for a police investigation," Barth was saying. "Scientists and eccentricity go together like—"

"He has never refused to see me. The people I spoke to at the War Department claim that he's suddenly forbidden all visitors, including his daughter. But that's just not like him."

Barth traded knowing looks with Cranston. "Maybe the new restrictions were issued by the War Department. After all, his work is classified, isn't it?"

"Of course, but it's not top secret, if that's what you mean. He's involved in energy research. Some kind of implosion device."

Cranston looked up sharply but turned away before Margo could notice.

"Something's wrong, Commissioner," she was saying. "I can feel it. When I spoke to him on the phone this morning, he was fine. But tonight he sounded distant and confused. And he was babbling in what sounded like *Chinese*."

Barth drained the last of his drink and motioned for a waiter.

Margo showed him a disapproving look and went on. "My father doesn't speak Chinese, Commissioner. What do I have to do, place an ad in the papers for The *Shadow* to help me?"

Barth grimaced, then sighed with purpose. "All right. I'll have someone drop by the Federal Building to see him. Will that suffice?"

Margo relaxed somewhat. "That's all I was asking for." But when she turned to solicit Cranston's opinion, he was no longer there. She glanced over her shoulder and saw him leaving the club. "Excuse me," she told Barth, getting to her feet and hurrying after him.

Cranston had collected his hat, scarf, and overcoat from the coat-check girl and was moving fast, but Margo was only steps behind him when he reached the sidewalk, the doormen under the awning gesturing good night with tips of their top hats. She tried calling to him, but he didn't stop; so she put some volume behind her second attempt. When he didn't respond even then, she quickened her pace and caught hold of his arm, bringing him around to face her.

"Wait a minute, will you?" she began. "What's your hurry? Did I say something to—"

She stopped herself, confronted by a look in his eye she hadn't met before, a burning look that didn't wear well on an alleged man about town. Suddenly there was nothing carefree about Lamont Cranston. He seemed filled with an almost vicious urgency. The force of his glare made her back away from him in alarm.

"Your eyes," she said, locked into his minatory gaze.

He held that gaze for a moment, then whirled and took a step toward the Cord taxi that had pulled up to the curb.

"Ying Ko," she said, not at all certain where the words had come from, what they meant, or what had made her blurt them out.

Cranston stopped short of the open rear door and did a slow turn.

Margo swallowed hard. Ying Ko sounded like a Chinese name. So was she beginning to speak in tongues like her father? Had both of them come down with some sort of contagious speech dysfunction? Cranston was eyeing her balefully.

"Who is Ying Ko?" she asked, still confused, but somehow sensing that Cranston knew or even *was* the answer.

His eyes were glowing blue orbs, boring into her. When he spoke, his voice had dropped in pitch and was seasoned with something sinister.

"You'll forget me."

She stared at him, wondering what he was up to now. "Not likely, Mr. Cranston. And why would I, anyway?"

"You'll give me no further thoughts," he went on in

that same low tone, showing her the red ring on his left hand.

Margo glanced at the ring and forced an aggravated exhale. "Look, Mr. Cranston, I don't know what kind of women you're used to dealing with, but I certainly don't appreciate—"

Cranston swung away from her. As he climbed into the Cord, the door seemed to shut itself, and the cab squealed into traffic, disappearing around the first corner. Completely baffled, Margo didn't make a move. She wasn't certain, but the cab driver looked like the same one who had driven them to her brownstone the night she and Cranston had met.

Shrevnitz heard the drawer beneath the seat open; then he caught a rearview mirror glimpse of The Shadow's broad-brimmed hat and neatly folded cloak. Cranston was breathing harshly and rapidly.

"The Federal Building," he said in a grating tone.

A sudden snap of the black cloak gave the hackie a start. The Shadow had melded into the darkened rear. Spooked, Shrevnitz readjusted the angle of the rearview and gave the car the gun.

"Hot dog?" inquired the shorter of the two Marine sentries posted at the door to Reinhardt Lane's lab. A sidelong glance revealed a torqued expression on his partner's face. "Well, I'm sure not gonna eat another hamburger."

"I'm not asking you to eat a hamburger," the taller Marine made clear.

The elevator at the end of the long hallway announced its arrival with a bright *ding*, and the two men peered at it, hands on holstered .45s. But when the doors opened, the car was empty. They looked at each other and shrugged.

"You like fried fish?" the first one asked.

His partner returned a noncommittal grunt. "What about a hamburger?"

The shorter man adopted a long-suffering look. Maybe he'd put in for that transfer to the South Pacific, after all. It wasn't like there was a war going on. He was about to say as much when he heard a *tsssicck*ing sound that ended with someone or something slamming him hard in the ribs. Looking down, he saw the wooden shaft of a leather-fletched arrow protruding from his chest. The "Oh" he managed was more one of surprise than pain. But his body knew that irreparable damage had been done to it, and his knees were already starting to buckle.

His partner looked at him with widened eyes; then the sound returned and instantly a like arrow was buried in his thorax. The Marines regarded one another in anguished dread, then, with moaning sighs, slumped to the ground. The last thing the second sentry saw was a group of swarthy Asians in helmets and archaic body armor standing in the elevator car.

At least one of them was armed with a crossbow.

Khan's right-hand man, Hoang Shu, led his charges into Lane's cluttered laboratory. The sword-bearing captain of the guard was built like an ironmolder, and wore a Fu Manchu style beard. Save for a foot-long ponytail at the back of his skull, his head was shaved. Clicks from Hoang Shu's tongue sent his cohorts fanning through the room, drawing swords, and opening folded crossbows.

Transfixed, Lane was standing to one side of his desk, methodically buttoning his tweed jacket. As instructed by the Llama billboard, he had placed the orb in a cushioned carrying case, the lid of which had reinforced corners and was stenciled with the words, WAR DEPARTMENT. On a click from Hoang Shu's tongue, Lane lifted the case by its handle.

But a sound from the balcony brought the Mongol to a sudden halt. Once more, he clicked his tongue at Lane, and the professor set the case down, resuming his motionless stance. Hoang Shu motioned one of the bowmen to check on the noise.

The bowman came through the balcony doors with his weapon raised in front of him and moved to the front wall, where he looked over the edge. Seeing and hearing nothing, he went to the wall opposite the billboard. As he was glancing about, his back to the wall of the building, black-gloved hands swooped down, as if out of nowhere, and grabbed hold of the conical crown of his helmet, yanking him off his feet.

The bowman screamed, more out of surprise than anything else, kicking booted feet in the air and losing hold of his weapon, which clattered to the balcony floor. His hands free, he reached above his head for the rigid wrists that were lifting him and put all his strength into a downward tug of his arms.

The Shadow flew headfirst from his perch on the roof ledge, executing a midair somersault; then, when his feet made contact with the balcony, a nimble forward roll placed him out of arm's reach of his opponent. The Mongol saw only a rolling ball of blackness until The

Shadow whirled on him, showing the upper mask of his ax-keen face. The Asian drew his saber and attacked, only to find The Shadow more than willing to meet him halfway. The two men struggled for dominance of the raised sword, until a right cross from The Shadow sent Asian and blade flying.

Before his armored adversary could recover, The Shadow stepped in, grabbing him in a forward-facing bear hug. He lifted him off his feet, flinging him through a half circle. But the Mongol was no slouch; he reversed the hold, answering The Shadow in kind, and landing him on his back atop the balcony's front wall.

While behind him, rings puffed from the mouth of the contented smoker, the Mongol pressed the attack, throwing himself on The Shadow and maneuvering him closer and closer to the edge. His back bent over the wall, The Shadow almost succeeded in squirming out from under the Asian. But all at once, the Mongol put the power of his stout legs into a final push, and over the two men went, locked in a deadly embrace.

12 Sciaphobia: Fear of Shadows

The Shadow was in the midst of calculating his rate of fall and terminal velocity when he and his aerial-act companion struck an unyielding surface that certainly wasn't the street. When he'd shaken off his momentary dislocation, The Shadow realized that they had, in fact, fallen less than two stories, landing on one of the Federal Building's architectural embellishments: a stone eagle with outstretched wings ten feet wide. Anticipating impact twenty-three stories below, The Shadow had rolled himself into a superior position, and so the Mongol—who was the better fortified for it, in any case—had taken the brunt of their crash, sustaining countless broken bones as a result. Just now, he lay facedown on the eagle's back, with The Shadow atop and astride him.

"Next time, you can be on top," The Shadow muttered through his scarf. He glanced skyward toward the balcony and began his ascent. Scaling the side of the building, he wished he had thought to bring along the suction devices he normally employed for such acts of death-defying dexterity, but time hadn't permitted it.

Inside Lane's laboratory, the rest of Khan's imperial guards were waiting in vigilant unease. Evidence of his controlling master's unfathomable powers, the professor himself was standing stock-still by his desk, psychically sealed off from the activity around him. Pausing outside the balcony doors, The Shadow melded with the lab's dim, flickering light and eased into the room.

Hoang Shu had his saber at the ready when a seemingly invisible force snapped his head back. Two follow-up blows from The Shadow's fists sent him reeling backward into a counter topped with glassware, most of which tipped over and shattered on the floor. The force of the punches dropped the Mongol as well, whose outstretched left arm swept a gooseneck lamp from its soapstone perch, further darkening the room.

The felling of their leader sent the other Asians into a frenzied counteroffensive. The glinting blades of curved swords sliced the air and hands and feet shot out in lightning-fast displays of Chinese martial arts techniques.

Back came The Shadow's attenuated laugh, wicked and taunting, though the laugh came from lips that could not be seen.

A gliding adumbration closed on the Mongol who was waving two swords about. The first punch left him stunned; the more forceful second stripped him of weapons. The Shadow sent him sprawling across another glass-filled countertop and down to the floor, where he landed in a confused heap, glancing up in wounded disbelief.

The three warriors who were still standing turned toward the general area of the attack, only to be left staggered by blows from fists, elbows, and knees. One's backward flailing carried him into a control panel, whose suddenly interrupted voltage took an instant liking to him. Held in the panel's galvanic grip, the armored warrior's arms, legs and head jerked spasmodically, while bolts of coruscating electricity danced around him.

Short-circuited, the lab's banks of overhead fluorescents went out. Shining through bubbling beakers, spirals of glass tubing, and racks of Erlenmeyer flasks, the countertop lights scattered chaotic shadows on the walls and ceiling.

The black-clad crimefighter was enjoying himself immensely, despite the rank smell the Mongols had introduced to the lab. (Springs represented the higher powers of their god, Tengri, so water was not permitted to be fouled by washing the body, clothes, cooking utensils, or dishes. That restriction and a steady diet of horse meat and fermented mare's milk contributed to a dizzying brew of odors.)

In fact, The Shadow was enjoying himself so much that he neglected to notice that the bald victim of his first blows, Hoang Shu, had risen to his feet and found his way to an ingenious idea. From the same countertop his fall had shaken, he had grabbed hold of a flashlight and was shining it around the now tenebrous room.

At first he saw nothing but his confederates stumbling back from the blows launched by their unseen assailant. But then Hoang Shu caught sight of something else: a streak of coiling blackness and a shadow on the far wall where there shouldn't have been one. The shadow showed the unmistakable silhouette of a tall man dressed in a high-collared cloak and broad-brimmed hat.

The sight brought a grin to the Asian's high-cheekboned face. Gripping the shaft of the Everready in his teeth, he raised his crossbow, nocked a quarrel, and aimed the loaded weapon.

Aware that the flashlight beam had betrayed him, The Shadow was darting left and right, but the Asian was successfully anticipating him. The Shadow heard the grind of the crank that drew back the bowstring; the racheting sound of the bow's three-arrowed, cylindrical quiver, which automatically rotated one of the bolts for nocking; the solid click of the locking nut; the loud snap of the trigger ...

He tried to toss himself outside of the beam, but the dartlike, leather-fletched arrow found the shoulder of the cloak and pinned it to a section of wall, which was papered with a Periodic Table. Encouraged, the bowman nocked a second arrow, adjusted his aim slightly, and fired once more, not only catching the cloak but a piece of The Shadow himself.

The Shadow grunted, then laughed shrilly. The Mongol's proficiency hadn't come as any surprise. Genghis Khan's bowmen were said to have been able to hit a man at a distance of 400 meters—on horseback.

By now the other Mongols had scrambled to their feet, praising Hoang Shu for his cleverness. But instead of partaking in the victory shout, one of the warriors was gesturing wildly to the wall, where The Shadow, weakened, was resolving into full visibility, pinned to the Periodic Table between Barium and Radon, like some insect specimen to a collector's tray.

Agog, Hoang Shu shouted a battle cry and nocked the bow's final arrow—the one apparently meant for the heart of his prey.

But The Shadow was also in motion, confident of his prowess. With the deftness of a gunslinger, his gloved hands crossed and dove beneath his cloak, reappearing an instant later clutching fistfuls of nickel-plated vengeance. The bowman froze, the war cry caught in his throat. Then the pumping muzzles of The Shadow's guns tongued their deadly hail, and two of the warriors fell. Hoang Shu and two others managed to dive for cover as the sledging automatics continued to spit hot lead and spew casings.

The Shadow uttered a whispered laugh. The superiority of bullets over arrows was once again proven.

Hearing the clicking of the depleted guns, Hoang Shu and another Mongol rose and made a mad dash for Reinhardt Lane and the encased implosion device. Even with fists, arrows, and bullets flying around him, the professor had stood passively throughout the fray, but he snapped to on Hoang Shu's frantic clicking and once more took the carrier in hand. The two Mongols grabbed him by the arms and began to hurry him toward the door.

The smoldering weapons reholstered, The Shadow tore himself free of the bodkin-tipped quarrels and was hot on the heels of the abductors when the sole remaining warrior tackled him, driving him sideways out the balcony doors.

The Shadow landed hard on his back but scurried to his feet in time to see the Asian lunging toward him with a raised dagger. The Mongol had lost his helmet in the lab, but a folded crossbow was still slung over his back. The Shadow ducked as his opponent rushed in, then threw him over his shoulder, sailing him out over the balcony wall.

The Asian, however, had managed to hook on to The Shadow's right arm and was nearly successful in pulling him off the balcony as well. It was only The Shadow's left hand that had saved him by latching on to the inner edge of the wall.

Facedown on top of the wall, his cloak unfurling in the wind, The Shadow's right arm was fully extended, his hand clamped on the Mongol's right wrist. Too, the dangling Mongol had the Shadow by the wrist. This time there was no eagle to break the fall.

The warrior twisted about, as if to drag The Shadow over the top. "Hold on," The Shadow told him. "Hold on or I'll let you die."

The Asian looked at him and grinned. "Die, yes," he said in guttural English. "The better to serve my Khan." Adopting an expression of blissful serenity, he relaxed his grip on The Shadow's wrist.

The muscles of The Shadow's hand and forearm flexed, but there was no holding onto the man. The Mongol worked himself free and plummeted, screaming, toward the street.

Twenty-five stories below, Shrevnitz was leaning on the rounded, right front fender of the Cord, wondering what was taking The Shadow so long. Moments earlier he thought he had glimpsed something on the eagle statue just below the top-floor balcony. But when he looked again, he saw nothing.

It was then he'd decided to push a bit further into the gift Shirl had given him for his birthday, a slim book called *Developing Psychic Ability*. The book was a series of exercises designed to bring out latent powers of telepathy, clairvoyance, telekinesis, and something called remote viewing. Shrevnitz was up to the exercise on clairvoyance, which involved closing your eyes, emptying your brain of everyday thoughts, and waiting to see what thoughts filled the empty space.

Just now he had his eyes closed in intense concentration when he heard a *whoosh*ing sound that he couldn't ignore. "Hey, I sense something coming," he said aloud.

But for some reason his eyes wanted to look up, directly over his head . . .

Where something was falling straight for him.

Shrevnitz flung himself out of the way at the last instant as an object crashed onto the street and fragmented into dozens of pieces. He walked over to the largest fragment and bent down to examine it. It was a piece of wood—walnut, maybe—from a bow of some kind.

While he was turning it about in his hand, a second object slammed to the sidewalk on the far side of the cab. Slammed with a viscous thud and a jangle of what sounded like chains.

Cautiously, Shrevnitz edged around the nose of the car. On the ground was the body of a man who could have stepped from a museum exhibit on ancient warfare. Shrevnitz glanced at the pieces of the bow, then back at the man. A shiver of dread ran through him, and he pulled his coat tightly to his neck as he made for the driver's seat.

He was just settling himself behind the steering wheel when a raspy voice from the rear said, "Drive."

Shrevnitz jumped and twisted around, finding The Shadow slumped in a corner, visibly drained and perhaps wounded. The hackie aimed a trembling forefinger in the direction of the sidewalk. "What the hell is that, boss?"

"A Mongol warrior. Strong, well trained."

Shrevnitz leaned toward the passenger-side window to regard the body. Then he shook his head, as if to clear it, and dropped the car into gear.

"Too bad they don't fly so good," he told The Shadow.

Shiwan Khan slouched sullenly in his throne, listening to Hoang Shu's report of the skirmish in Lane's laboratory. Five of his best men had been lost, reducing the imperial guard to a little better than half its former strength. The thought of importing additional warriors left him cold.

"It could only be Ying Ko," he said, rising. "None other could have cloaked himself as he did."

Hoang Shu bowed his head.

Khan mulled it over as he came down the stairs. When he finally spoke it wasn't to his lieutenant, but to the still transfixed Professor Lane, who was standing between Hoang Shu and a second Mongol, from whose hands hung the carrying case.

"You must begin work at once. I want the device readied in forty-eight hours."

"Yes, my Khan," Lane said, reaching for the case.

Khan regarded him for a moment. He had first learned of Lane's research from a physicist in China. That same scientist had speculated that Lane's search for a new energy source was nothing more than disinformation perpetuated by America's War Department. Surely, Lane was at work on a bomb, which lacked only a suitable fuel—one that China's own desert wastes could supply in abundance to Shiwan Khan. Lane, however, was only half the answer.

The professor had turned to leave the throne room

when Khan bade him stop. "Before you go, there's something I need you to do."

Lane straightened obediently.

"I want you to make a telephone call." Khan narrowed his gaze. "And be certain that my instructions are followed to the letter."

Margo tapped her foot impatiently as the elevator rose slowly to the twenty-fifth floor of the Federal Building. She had just walked into her apartment when her father had phoned to say that he needed to see her. He'd said he was fine, but he hadn't sounded it. Especially when he added that he needed to see her at the lab—immediately.

That was close to an hour ago, and ever since she had been trying to fight down gnawing concern. But at least he was willing to see her. Which meant that Commissioner Barth was wrong about the War Department having issued the "no visitors" restrictions. And he wasn't speaking *Chinese*.

First, Lamont Cranston storming out of the Cobalt Club for no apparent reason; then that "Ying Ko" business on the sidewalk; and now a call out of the blue from her father. It was shaping up to be quite a night.

The elevator chimed, and the doors slid open. Margo hurried into the hallway only to stop dead in her tracks several doors short of 2512. The two Marine sentries were dead—with arrows projecting from their chests!

She put her hand to her mouth and forced herself to keep walking. And to step over the bodies.

"Dad?" she yelled, coming through the open door to the lab.

Even in the faint, flickering light she could see that

some horrible struggle had taken place. There were two more bodies on the floor, riddled with bullet wounds. Then another body—strangely costumed in Oriental silk and armor. But no sign of her father.

"Dad, where are you?" she said in rising panic. She went to the open balcony doors. "Please be here," she said to herself.

The balcony was empty, save for a sword and a bulky crossbow. She stared at the weapons in dismay. What in god's name had gone on? Where was her father?

Something drew her attention to the Llama billboard on the building across the street. She walked to the wall and spent a long moment watching the smoke rings. What with the lights and all, the rings could produce an almost hypnotic effect if you stared at them for too long. . . . Her eyes refocused on the face of the contented smoker himself, but the face had undergone a change. It was an Asian face that seemed to be gazing at her.

She wanted to turn away, but she couldn't convince her legs to move. Then a voice made her look at the sign again. The lips of the Asian were moving. *"Margo Lane,"* they were saying. *"You have been living a lie. . . ."*

13 Chinatown

In his bedroom in the Cranston mansion, The Shadow, wearing a sleeveless white undershirt, dressed the arrow gash in his shoulder. In his years of battling crime he had sustained wounds from handguns, chatterboxes, brass knuckles, saps, fists, feet, and the lumpy foreheads of assorted gunzels and gorillas; but an arrow wound was something new. The short-shafted quarrel had cut a three-inch-long groove in the top of his right deltoid, shallow but somewhat ragged around the edges. Nothing, however, that would require the services of Dr. Rupert Sayre, recruited by The Shadow after being rescued from the clutches of "The Master of Death."

The manse was quiet, the staff asleep in their quarters. Cranston had most of the lights turned off. He was seated in amber light, in an armchair next to a round table, with the dressings beside him. If he chose to, he could watch himself in the full-length looking-glass directly across the room.

Marpa Tulku used to be able to close his wounds with the power of concentrated thought. For one trained, blood could be directed to or away from an infected or wounded area as need be; warmth could be brought to bear, the body temperature locally increased. Cranston made some use of those techniques now.

at her hands, as if they should have been holding something. "And I came here."

Cranston turned away from her to get control of himself. It was certainly more than "a voice" that had put the pistol into her hands. Like the coin, it was another message from Khan: Khan's way of indicating how vulnerable The Shadow was to exposure. He grabbed his shirt from the clothes rack, pulled it on, and whirled on her. "Then why did you come *here*?"

"I—I don't know."

He worked his jaw. "Get out."

She spied a bottle of bourbon on the desk and rushed to it, pouring a tumblerful and downing it in one swallow. "I don't even know how I got here."

"Go. Now."

"I came to kill The Shadow . . . and there was only you." She regarded him with sudden suspicion. Emboldened, she said, "Show me your eyes—the way they were on the street tonight."

He grinned menacingly as he backed her toward the door once more. "You want to see into my eyes?" He took her by the shoulders and shoved her lightly. "Go ahead, look at them."

"I know something," Margo was saying. "I knew before—"

"Look at them!"

Margo was shaking her head at him. "Something strange about you. I could feel it—"

Cranston was only a foot from her now. "But I've got to warn you, you won't like what you see."

"That static in my head. Whenever I was near you. I knew, I knew—"

"You're in danger," Cranston growled.

The color drained from her face. "You're The Shadow. You're *The Shadow*."

Cranston's face contorted. He balled up his left hand and threw it at her.

Margo shut her eyes, bracing herself for the impact of his fist. But instead, his blow whizzed past her left ear and struck the door panel. Open-handed. Then, just as quickly as he had grabbed her, he released her and re-coiled to the center of the room, shaking his hand. His behavior confused her, this sudden show of, what ... mercy? Shame? Perhaps because of what the world had learned of him over the years—the violence, the many deaths.

Margo was trembling uncontrollably. But she had a clear memory of the evening now: the phone call from her father, the trip to his lab, the dead Marines, the mayhem.... The last thing she recalled was stepping out onto the balcony and staring at the cigarette adver-tisement. Then, then ...

She tensed as a memory that didn't seem to belong to her blossomed into consciousness. The memory of an Asian man dressed in robes. His hands on her bare back as he had slipped the black stole from her shoulders. Her father displaying a wooden case that held the dueling pistol. The bullet the Asian had inserted into the chamber ... Margo's eyes darted to her hands, as if she were still holding the thing. Shiwan Khan, she thought, remembering herself speaking his name while she was on the laboratory balcony. Was he responsible for the killings at the lab? Had he abducted her father?

She looked at Cranston, who was buttoning his shirt and averting his gaze. She was frightened of how he would react, but she knew she had to get to him, to make the most of the moment.

"My father has disappeared from the lab. I was there. There were signs of a horrible fight. I went out onto the balcony, and that's when I heard the voice in my head. I think it was someone named Khan who took my father and sent me here to kill you. I'm afraid to go to the police. If you really are The Shadow, you're the only one who can help me find him."

Cranston turned to regard her with a mix of cruelty and sadness. "Don't be here when I get back," he warned. He started for the door, but she blocked his path.

"How do you know I won't tell anyone who you really are?" She tried to make it sound convincing.

Cranston got up in her face again, glaring at her. "I know," he seethed.

And this time, she knew better than to follow him.

While The Shadow had devoted the previous five years to perfecting his physical skills, Cranston told himself, Shiwan Khan had been devoting himself to perfecting the craft of psychic concentration. How else to explain the apparent ease with which he had remotely hypnotized the Lanes? If The Shadow was going to thwart Khan the way he had other archfiends of crimedom—men like the Brothers of Doom, the Green Hoods, the Gray Fist, and the Silent Seven—Cranston would have to prepare his mind for the coming battle. And what better place to do that than the subterranean headquarters, his cave, his chamber of solitude.

He was in the rear of Shrevnitz's cab, and they were closing on the Times Square alley that afforded access to the sanctum. It was almost midnight, and the city had been rained on again. Still seething over the encounter with Margo—not the attempt at murder but her threat to unmask him—he had said little to the hackie since climbing into the Cord five minutes earlier. Shrevnitz was accustomed to the brooding silences, however ... the silences and much worse.

Just now, the hackie's eyes kept moving to the rear-view mirror, but not, apparently, to check on Cranston.

"What it is, Shrevvy?" he asked at last.

"Something I don't like about the black-and-yellow behind us. I saw it on Fifty-third when we were leaving the house. That's why I've been taking the long route to Broadway. But this bird's following my every move." He turned to look over the seat back. "I think we've got a tail."

Cranston took him at his word. "All right, let's take him on a tour of downtown. If he's still with us by the time we reach Canal Street, pull over and let me out."

Shrevnitz nodded and increased speed, angling the taxicab back toward the East Side. The tail stayed with them, all the way south on Park, Second, then Bowery, until they were almost in Chinatown. Cranston got out near Canal, across the street from a funeral home, and continued walking south, stopping once to give a downward tug to his homburg—and to glance into the side mirror of a parked car. Less than a block behind him was one of Khan's underlings. That the man was in full battle regalia suggested that Cranston was meant to make him.

Another of Shiwan Khan's tests, Cranston thought, back in motion once more. Just down the street was a bakery, and just past that a dark, recessed doorway.

Quickening his pace, he cut diagonally across the wide sidewalk; then, employing a Hawkeye maneuver, he made a sudden right into the doorway and cloaked himself in the inky blackness. The Mongol's bootsteps became urgent, but by the time he reached the doorway, Cranston had disappeared. Nonplussed—or at least pretending to be—Khan's man hurried away, seemingly unaware of the black pool that gathered itself from the door and began to glide down the street behind him.

The Cord followed at a discreet distance.

The Mongol didn't turn until he had reached Pell Street, in the heart of Chinatown; then he veered west under a flat arch onto a short street bustling with pre–Chinese New Year activity, even at the late hour. Firecrackers pinwheeled on the support posts of the arch. People crowded around tables spread with exotic fruits and vegetables, Peking ducks, eels, birds' nests, and live turtles—for soup. Grinning tourists and uniformed soldiers mingled shoulder to shoulder with Asians hawking goose paté, fish, incense sticks, and assorted fireworks. Red lanterns hung from ropes strung between overhead balconies. The air smelled of saffron, gunpowder, moldy eggs, and roasted suckling pig.

Cranston was familiar with the area, because The Shadow had had dealings with a merchant named Loo Look, proprietor of a shop on Pell and Mott that sold tourist junk.

Fifty yards along, where a group of women were butchering fattened geese, the Mongol climbed the stairs to the Sun Yet Kitchen. Cranston stayed with him.

On the wall at the top of the stairs was a coiled firehose, and to the left of that the beaded entry to the restaurant itself. Cranston parted the curtain and had a look inside: a columned interior, red-tiled floor, an empty cashier's booth off to one side, a kitchen to the other—steam issuing from pots. There were a dozen tables, unoccupied save for one in the rear. Attended to by a waiter in pajamas and a skullcap, Shiwan Khan sat hunched over a plate of what looked like meat and goat cheese. He wore a dark blue Brooks Brothers suit and was eating with his right hand. His long hair glistened with pomade. The Mongol who had led the way to the rendezvous was nowhere to be seen.

"Nice tie," Cranston commented on approaching the table. It was the exact tie he had been wearing when Khan turned up in the sanctum.

Khan looked up from his plate and wiped his mouth with the back of his hand. "Thank you. Hasn't it been said that imitation is the sincerest form of flattery?"

"Too bad you aren't interested in imitating my good deeds."

"Or you my bad ones." Khan motioned to the chair opposite his.

Cranston removed his gloves and placed them, along with his hat and coat, on a neighboring table. "Not quite the headquarters I'd imagined for a prepotent conqueror."

Khan's eyes narrowed. "This isn't my headquarters."

"Oh, no? Then where *are* you located?"

Khan laughed. "Must you take the fun out of everything?"

Cranston rocked his head from side to side. "It was you who sent Professor Lane's daughter to kill me, wasn't it? Just so I'm clear on that point."

"Kill you, Ying Ko?" Khan snorted. "If I wanted you dead, I would be dining on your liver instead of this hunk of meat. No, I sent the meddlesome woman *to be killed*. You did kill her?"

"Sorry to disappoint you. She's alive and well."

Khan looked concerned. "Then she's a danger to you. She knows your identity." A rueful smile took shape. "I wonder how long Ying Ko will allow her to go on living? How long before his pure survival instincts assert control?"

Cranston leaned forward conspiratorially. "I know your plan, Khan. The bronzium, Lane's implosion device ... But you still don't have an initiator or a containment sphere. And without those, there's no bomb." He leaned closer still. "Besides, you know I'll stop you."

"You'll fail."

Cranston's nostrils flared. "The Shadow never fails."

Khan wiped his hands and mouth with a napkin and sat back in the chair. "You Americans are so confident. You think of your decadent nation as the new cradle of civilization. But let me remind you of one thing: the civilization that rules in one era is the manure for the next."

Cranston aimed a finger at him in melodramatic admonishment. "That's the U.S. of A. you're talking about, pal."

Khan scoffed at the notion. "The Doctrine of the Mandate of Heaven allows for the presumption that the fall of one dynasty and the accession of another is in itself evidence that the mandate has passed from one to the next. You talk of patriotism, nationalism, *jingoism*, when I'm talking about ruling the world!"

Cranston regarded him calmly and reached into his jacket pocket for his cigarette case and lighter. "I'd like to give you a name—Dr. Leonard Levinsky. Brilliant psychiatrist. Specializes in paranoia, delusions of grandeur, that sort of thing. You talk, he listens. I think you'll feel a lot better when you get some of these delusions off your—"

Khan bristled. "Your impudence is boring me!" Without warning he drew an unwieldy dagger from beneath the table and made a stab for Cranston's hand.

Cranston, however, had calculated the trajectory of the tip and spread his fingers to accommodate its passage into the hardwood tabletop.

"Most impressive," Khan said with mock sincerity.

Cranston's eyes went to the ruthless face carved into the handle of the triple-bladed knife.

Khan deciphered the look and smiled, leaving the *phurba* where it stood. "I'm glad to see that you recognize it, Ying Ko—even if you do seem to have forgotten everything else about your life in Tibet. Yes, I took it from Marpa Tulku. No, allow me to amend that. I took it *out* of him. After I ran it through his heart."

Hearing of the murder of his teacher, Cranston took hold of the *phurba* with both hands, yanking it from the table, feeling its power spread into his arms. But no sooner had he raised it to plunge into Khan, than the thing came alive as it had years earlier, the snarling face snapping at his flesh, until it had sunk its teeth deep into his wrist.

14 Chasing the Dragon

Cranston's pained cry brought a smile to Khan's face.

"That's right, you never did master the *phurba*." Khan shot the dagger a look, and it scooted obediently across the table on its tip into his hand. "You still expect it to respond to brute force. When will you learn to control your baser instincts?"

"Instincts?" Cranston said. "I'll show you instincts!" He lunged across the table, grabbing Khan by the throat with his uninjured hand. He was squeezing for all it was worth when he felt the cold touch of a gun barrel against his temple.

Khan's guard backed away when Cranston released his hold. But the Mongol remained close at hand, showing twin .38s. Khan was breathing hard, though none the worse for wear.

"My warriors aren't terribly bright," he said, massaging his throat. "But they are loyal."

Cranston relaxed in the chair, directing a concentrated sidelong look at the guard, whose heavy brow began to furrow in response.

"Accept the truth, Ying Ko," Khan was saying. "Without light there is no shadow, and, together, we *are* that shadow."

Cranston said nothing. The guard was struggling to

maintain his stance in the face of Cranston's psychic assault.

"I would sooner destroy a Rembrandt or a Ming Dynasty treasure than kill you, Ying Ko, but I promise I will—here, *now*—unless you give me the answer I crave. For the last time: are you with me or against me?"

Cranston only grinned. The guard had caught the headache he'd thrown and was biting down hard on his lip.

Khan returned the grin. "You can't defeat me, you know. Or fool me. Your mind is an open book."

Cranston finally glanced at him. "I'm sick of hearing that."

He leapt from his seat, turning toward the guard, who—with an expression of unmitigated anguish—tossed him one of the revolvers.

Shiwan Khan was nothing if not quick, however. He upended the table, throwing Cranston to one side before he could draw a bead on Khan. When he looked again, Khan had torn the second .38 from his minion's shaking grip.

"Weakling," he snarled, plunging the *phurba* into the man's chest and withdrawing it.

Cranston shot to his feet and took aim, in what amounted to a duelist's stance. Across the room, Khan mirrored the pose. And at the same moment, they fired.

The two bullets raced from the barrels, spiraling toward their destinations—which happened to be the hearts of Cranston and Shiwan Khan—but instead of hitting either, they collided in midair, the combined force of their kinetic energy fusing them into a disk three inches around, which dropped to the tile floor and spun there for a moment, like a top, before flattening itself.

Cranston alone was awed by the event. Khan was already on his way out of the room. And why settle for the stairs when, with little more than a gaze, you could blow out an entire window?

On the busy street below, waiting with hands thrust into the pockets of his peacoat, Moe Shrevnitz heard glass shatter and feared for a moment that another Mongol warrior might be plummeting toward him. Then he realized that the sound had come from the Sun Yet Kitchen, which Cranston had entered several minutes earlier, and that just now a suited figure was executing a near perfect front layout through what remained of a blown-to-pieces double-hung window.

Fleeing shards of flying glass, a knot of Asians and tourists were scattering, dropping sacks, baskets, tools, and trays of food, intent on clearing a space for the figure that was dropping into their midst.

Clutching a bayonetlike dagger in one hand, the figure landed neatly on his feet. Shrevnitz saw that it wasn't Cranston but someone of comparable acrobatic grace. And more than that, someone with a network of agents comparable to that of The Shadow. For even as the hackie watched, a motorcycle with an attached sidecar was roaring onto the scene, another one of those Mongol warriors in the driver's saddle.

The bike was a big-engined, maroon BMW, with gold dragon detailing on the fenders and the filigreed head and backrests. What appeared to be machine guns were mounted under the chariot and low down on the right-hand side of the engine.

No sooner had the jumper settled into the sidecar than the driver stomped the machine into gear and sped off, slaloming through skidding left and right turns. But by then, Shrevnitz was already running for the Cord, which was parked at the end of the short block, just beyond the arch.

Cranston was waiting outside the Sun Yet Kitchen when the hackie pulled up. He slid into the back seat. Shrevnitz dropped the front-wheel-drive cab into gear and squealed into the same rain-slicked turns the motorcycle had taken. Once on the straightaway, he stomped on the gas pedal.

Up ahead, the Mongol was maneuvering his machine through Chinatown's narrow streets with little concern for pedestrians. Some were lucky enough to leap to the safety of sidewalks or the roofs of parked cars, but some weren't and they were tossed into the air like rag dolls.

Shrevnitz, in operative mode, had both eyes on the road, both hands viced on the wheel, and was doing his best to gain on the bike without adding to the body count. But there were things a bike could do and places it could go that a sedan couldn't—even one in the hands of a skilled driver.

"Ten to one that driver's from Jersey," Shrevnitz told Cranston.

Determined to catch up, Shrevnitz leaned over the wheel and sent the gas pedal to the floor, only to see a couple of winos come staggering into the street from between two parked cars.

Shrevnitz pounced on the brake and managed to bring the Cord to a shuddering stop just short of the bum holding the bottle. Swaying in the middle of the street, oblivious to any danger, the wino glanced at the car, then passed the bottle to his chum, who took a slug and passed it back. The guy then offered it to Shrevnitz, who shook his head in anger and motioned them to move out of the street. Which they did, in their own good time, waving the Cord by, with gallant bows and a sweep of their arms.

It was a loss now, and both Shrevnitz and Cranston knew it. Regardless, the hackie took up the chase. But there was nothing but dark, empty street, illuminated by blobs of yellow light. Luncheonettes, flophouses, and converted speakeasys on either side, except for a stretch of vacant lot on the northeast corner of Second and Houston.

The rubble-strewn lot was a block behind them when Cranston told Shrevnitz to turn the Cord around. Shrevnitz thought that maybe he'd caught a glimpse of the cycle on one of the side streets, but after he'd completed the U-turn, Cranston told him to pull up across the street from the lot itself.

Cranston climbed out and went to the wire mesh that surrounded the lot, and stared at the masonry debris and trash as if something didn't add up. But damned if Shrevnitz could figure it out; to him, it was just a place where a building had been. After a while, Cranston returned to the rear seat, but he didn't talk about what he'd been thinking, and Shrevnitz didn't ask.

The mansion was dark, but someone had built a fire in the den's fireplace. One of the servants, perhaps, anticipating that his employer might opt to sleep on the couch, as was often his habit. Cranston, in fact, had it in mind to do just that, but when he arrived at the couch he found it already occupied.

Margo was asleep on her back, her face turned away

from the fire. Sensing him standing there, she sat up, rubbing her eyes.

"I can't help what I know about you," she said before he could say anything. "But I can't forget it, either. My father is all I have in the world, and right now, you're all he has."

Cranston's emotions were mixed. While he wanted to turn on her for ignoring his demands, he couldn't deny being mildly relieved at discovering her there, safe, and, more importantly, *unarmed*. "I'll do what I can," he told her. "But alone."

"Why? Just because that's always been your way of operating? You have to admit we have a connection of some kind. So why can't I help you?"

He shook his head, wanting to say that she'd only be in the way. But what he said was, "You wouldn't be safe with me." Which was certainly true, in any case. "You could be hurt."

She seemed almost entertained by the idea. "By you? I don't think you're capable of that."

His eyes narrowed. "You have no idea what I'm capable of." He swung away from her and stepped up onto the brick hearth. When he turned to face her, the firelight caught the planes and angles of his face.

"I was thirteen years old the first time it happened. One morning at school a cousin of mine—from the good side of the family, the one with money—divulged that I'd cheated on a test. I had cheated, but his betrayal infuriated me. I didn't say anything when he talked, but I caught up with him after school, in the bathroom, figuring I'd teach him a lesson."

Cranston took a few steps toward her, acting out the part now. "I remember it vividly. I grabbed hold of him, and I knocked him to the floor. Then I put my hands around his throat, and I started choking the life out him. His face began to turn purple. His arms were waving—hard at first, then hardly at all. I could see the fear in his eyes and I could smell it coming off him like a scent."

He threw Margo a glimlet glance, realizing from her curled posture that he was getting to her. "I found his panic ... extraordinary. The fact is, I'd never felt power like that before—the power of life and death." He returned to the fire, his expression darkening, contorting his entire face. "I knew that something inside me had revealed itself. Some beastlike thing that fed on violence. An ugly, diabolic thing that was trying to claw its way to the surface and take control."

He glanced at Margo again. "No, I didn't kill him. The beast was controllable then. I left my handsome, blond cousin gasping for breath on the floor of the bathroom. But I left him alive. I went to the sink and splashed water on my face. And when I happened to look in the mirror it was as if I could see the face of the thing inside me, the thing that was sharing my body. . . ."

"As I got older, I tried to run from it—from myself—but it was no good. I enlisted so I could fight in the war, thinking I could appease the thing. But war only made matters worse. Afterward ... Well, eventually I ended up in the Far East, and what I became there I don't want you or anyone else to know about. But there was someone there who could see both my faces, and with his help I retrieved the face I'd been born with. He helped me redirect the beast's power—or at least he helped me harness its power so that the beast and I could both have our way."

Cranston loosed a sardonic laugh. "Don't get the

wrong idea. My teacher didn't see me as some kind of holy reincarnation of a dead lama. He saw me for just what I was—a malevolent force that could be redeemed and made to do good." He looked hard at Margo. "Tonight I learned that my teacher was murdered by the same man who abducted your father and sent you here to kill me."

He didn't dare tell her the truth: that she'd been sent to *be* killed.

Margo started to speak, but he cut her off.

"I'm no different from the malefactors I bring to justice. What I do is done to placate the evil in me, because it hasn't left me. Some part of it is still here—in my heart—waiting for an opportunity to take control again. Ready and willing to hurt people. Maybe even the ones I love."

After a long moment of waiting for him to continue, Margo asked, "Is there someone you love?"

Cranston stared coldly at her, resistant as steel. "No."

"Then how do you know those close to you are in jeopardy?"

She got up off the divan and began to move toward him, cautiously. Cranston held his ground. She moved closer, raising her arms, reaching out to him—

He grabbed hold of her hands and held her away from him. The fire crackled, its flames reflected in the red stone of his ring.

"It's late," he said. "Sleep here if you want, but there are plenty of guest rooms upstairs. Either way, I don't want to see you here in the morning."

"I'm not afraid of you," she said bravely.

Cranston's eyes clouded over. "That's all right. I'm afraid enough for both for us."

15 Mind Games

Cranston lay awake in bed, fully clothed.

Restless for something he couldn't discern, he climbed from bed, leaving the master bedroom and stealing down the darkened hallway to the guest room Margo Lane had selected. Finding the door unlocked, he let himself in. The room was warm, and Margo's sleeping form was loosely tangled in the bed clothes, one shapely, naked leg revealed. Gazing at her, he found himself torn, but between what he couldn't decide. And so, instead, he crossed the room to a bureau, over which hung a large mirror. A shaded lamp on the bureau illuminated his reflection.

He stood regarding himself for a long moment, before becoming aware of a smudge on his cheek, the sort that might have been left by one's finger after reading a newspaper. But when he tried to erase the smudge it didn't fade. Not even when he wet his thumb and rubbed at the spot. Rather, it began to increase in size and change from ink black to irritated red.

He went after the spot with a vengeance now, really rubbing at it and, at the same time, growing vaguely apprehensive. To his horror, he realized that he had rubbed away a patch of skin!

He held the bloody strip in his hand, sickened by the

sight of it. But that was only the beginning. Gazing at himself once more, he discovered that the rubbing had revealed a glimpse of something adhering to the bone beneath the patch. With growing dismay, he started to peel away the skin, slipping his fingers underneath the edges, determined to expose the scope of what was hidden. His bloody fingers attacked his face with increasing speed, wedging themselves into places they had no right being, yanking off his nose, his lips and eyelids, as if extricating himself from a flesh mask . . . Until at last there was no skin remaining, save for that belonging to the face that underlaid his own.

That of Shiwan Khan—

A terrified scream from Margo brought him about-face. She was sitting upright, staring at him, pulling the sheets to her neck. Driven by some vague compulsion, his hands reached for the dagger he hadn't noticed on the bureau until just then. It was, of course, the *phurba*. Raising it, he took aim at her heart and hurled it—

The nightmare had the mercy to release Cranston before the blade struck its target.

In bed once more, the dreamer raised himself on his elbows until he was sitting up, bathed in sweat and panting with dread.

Sunlight streaming through French windows woke her. The unfamiliarity of her surroundings troubled her until her mind put things in proper order: she was in one of the mansion's guest rooms, having given up on getting a good night's rest on the couch in the den. She was in her slip on an ornate four-poster, and some time during the night had worked her way out from under a burgundy satin comforter. The comforter matched the carpet, the window drapes, and a silk chair near the fireplace. The bed had a dust ruffle, and at its foot sat a brocaded bench. There were candlesticks, bibelots, and a brass clock on the mantel, and, above it, an oil portrait of a stern-faced woman of sixty or so. Off to the right of the bed stood a bird's-eye maple wardrobe; the linen lace showing in the doors was repeated in the panels of a nearby dressing screen. A vanity with an oval mirror, a Louis XV commode, a chiffonier red and white flowers atop tall pedestals ...

The room's fin-de-siècle elegance brought to mind the house in Chicago she had lived in until her mother had died. ... Renewed concern for her father crowded into her thoughts; then the late-night conversation with Lamont Cranston—*The Shadow.* She recalled the cruel look in his eye, his warning that she shouldn't overstay her welcome. She rolled over on her left side and fluffed the pillows under her head. An unfinished dream lulled her back to sleep while she was deciding just what she should do about Cranston.

She couldn't have been asleep more than a minute when her eyes opened. Cranston, dressed in a dark blue chalk-striped suit, was standing by the bed. "Good morning," he said.

"Good morning to you," she told him, encouraged by his pleasant tone. She yawned, stretched, and pushed her hair from her face, making no move to cover herself. "God, did I dream."

Interested, he sat down on the edge of the bed. "Really? So did I. What went on in yours?"

She rolled over on her back and closed her eyes for a moment, eager to grasp the dream before it fled to that place from which there was no retrieving it. "I was on a beach somewhere. In the South Seas, maybe. I was naked, and the waves were just covering my toes." Provocatively, she ran her hand along her body to her face and lowered her voice to a sexy whisper. "The sun was beating down on me, but my skin seemed to be cool and hot at the same time. It felt wonderful." She took a deep breath and looked at him. "What did you dream?"

"That I ripped the flesh off my face and found someone else's face underneath," he said matter-of-factly.

She dropped the seductive act and straightened somewhat against the headboard. "You have problems."

"I'm aware of that." He got up and started for the door. "I'll wait outside while you dress."

"No, that's okay," she said quickly. "You can stay." She climbed from the bed and went to where she had tossed her cut-velvet dress and stole. Cranston, the gentleman, all of a sudden, averted his gaze. Sort of.

Maybe there was a man inside him, after all, she thought. But further testing was required. She regarded the ensemble with embroidered dismay. "Oh, these are all rumpled."

Cranston glanced at the dress, then her, then walked around the bed to the wardrobe. "There are some things in here that might fit. They belong to . . . my Aunt Rose. She stays here sometimes."

Hardly matronly, the garment he showed her was a sheer black satin charmeuse, open in the back and belted, with a keyhole opening at the neckline. The label showed that it had come from Natacha Rambova, on East Fifty-second Street. A glance at the other garments hanging in the wardrobe revealed them to be equally haute couture.

"Quite the fashion plate, my Aunt Rose," Cranston said, as if reading her thoughts.

Margo held the frock to herself. "She's obviously kept her figure, as well." Dress in hand, she disappeared behind the changing screen. The clothes seemed to bear out the rumors about Cranston the ladies' man. But just how much of his cavorting had been perpetrated to maintain appearances? she wondered.

"Listen," he was saying from the other side of the screen, "I've got a—"

"—taxi waiting downstairs?" she completed. It would have been a safe bet, but the words really had popped into her mind. She poked her head from behind the screen to regard him. "That *is* what you were about to say, isn't it?"

"Yes," he said, clearly peeved. "But—"

"Hey, this telepathy business is getting easier the more I'm around you. You're like reading a book." She shrugged out of her slip and draped it over the top of the screen where he couldn't help but notice it. Or her, with the light streaming in through the windows behind her.

Cranston was quiet for a long moment, then said. "About the cab—"

"Well, thank you very much, but I don't need it."

"Yes, you do. I have things—"

"Great. I'll come with you."

"Excuse me?"

She poked her head from behind the screen once more. "I'll come with you."

"No. Last night we agreed—"

"I didn't agree to anything," she interrupted in a rush. "Do you mind if I just get one short sentence out here, thank you very much. Last night we both agreed that you were going to leave this morning."

She slipped into the dress. "No, *you* agreed I was going to leave. I agreed to no such thing." She looked at him and forced a sure smile. "We need each—"

The Shadow's laugh interrupted, wordless but more expressive than a statement. "No, we don't."

"We have a connection."

"No, we don't."

"Then how do you explain that I can read your thoughts?"

"My thoughts are hard to miss."

"And why's that?"

"Psychically, I'm very well endowed."

She laughed shortly and gave him a quick once-over. "I'll bet you are." She disappeared to finish dressing. "Okay, so you don't need me. But I need you. And if your present plans happen to include finding out what's happening to my father, then I'm coming with you. All he knows is his research. He's helpless away from the lab. He can't even tell red from green, much less escape from Shiwan Khan."

She emerged from behind the screen, confident that the dress made her look like a million. And, indeed, the human side of The Shadow was drinking her in.

She smiled, and exhaled. "So, where do we start?"

He cocked an eyebrow. "Suppose you tell me."

It was a wonderful day for sightseeing: mild temperature, clear skies, hardly any wind. Shiwan Khan and his eminently suggestible subject, Reinhardt Lane, stood on the uppermost observation deck of the Empire State Building, one thousand feet above the city streets.

The observation deck of the five-year-old, largely empty skyscraper had played host to sky parties, wedding ceremonies, seances, lovers' trysts, visits by horses and minicars, and radio broadcasts by the RKO Theater of the Air. With the wind currents born in the surrounding canyons, it often snowed *up* at the top, and sometimes *red*, owing to dust particles adhering to the flakes. In the past, the observation deck had been bombarded by pellets of barley launched from the Great Plains, and insects indigenous to areas fifteen hundred miles away. The tower itself—planned as a mooring mast for dirigibles—had even served as a battlement for a giant ape.

Looking south, one could see across the lower part of Manhattan Island and New York Harbor clear to the ocean. North—the direction Khan and Lane were facing—were the black ribbons of roadways, a miniature Central Park, the apartment houses of the Bronx and Queens.

How different from his native Mongolia, Shiwan Khan was telling himself. The Altai and Tien Shan mountain ranges, the Gobi, the vast forests of Siberia. Baked in summer, frozen in winter . . .

Lane, wearing his brown wool tweed suit, had one arm outstretched to the horizon. "From there . . . to there," he said, describing a 180-degree arc that began in the hills of Westchester and ended beyond the Palisades of the Hudson River.

Khan, in his gold-beaded robe and a black-fur Mandarin cap, was visibly impressed. "That will be the range of destruction?"

Lane shook his head. A biplane was circling in the near distance. Overhead, the federal and state flags snapped in the wind. "That's simply a rough estimate of the blast radius of the explosion. The destruction will extend well into the suburban areas. What with the shock wave and the firestorm, it's impossible to predict the extent of the damage."

"Ah, what a day," Khan said in unabashed delight.

The curious cadence of the professor's monotone might have puzzled anyone within earshot, but the observation deck wasn't especially crowded at that time of day, just thirty or so tourists, bundled up in overcoats and hats, some with their own binoculars, others huddled around the deck's several viewing scopes. Children scurried about, waving souvenir banners of New York City or the city's baseball teams; elsewhere were groups of sailors on shore leave, in peajackets and caps.

A group of four sailors off the USS *Texas* walked past Khan and Lane. One of the group, a young man with thick eyebrows and swarthy good looks, felt obliged to comment on Khan's costume. "Nice dress, toots," he told the would-be ruler of the world. When Khan glared in indignation, the sailor blew him a kiss, which set everyone laughing.

Khan was not amused. Raising the fore and middle fingers of his left hand, he sent the sailor a minor reprimand. An easy prey, the sailor stopped short while his shipmates continued on their way to a corner viewing scope. Khan made a fist of his right hand and made beckoning motions with his left. The sailor turned and scampered to the top of the observation deck's four-foot-high wall. A few more manual commands from Khan, and the visibly confounded sailor had scaled the eight-foot-high fence that crowned the wall. The fence had been added to deter potential leapers, since the suicide of a pretty but despondent young woman shortly after the building had been dedicated.

By then, people had observed the sailor's actions and were pointing and gesticulating in helpless concern. A woman in a fur hat fainted, and someone knelt down to fan her with a tourist information leaflet. Others whirled away, terror-stricken by the sailor's precarious hold on the blunt bars that comprised the fence. At last, one of his shipmates noticed him and alerted the rest.

"Bobby!" someone yelled. "What the hell are you doing?"

Bobby swung him a panicked look. "I got no idea! Jeezus, get me down from here! Get me down!"

The only person watching Shiwan Khan was a young kid in a brimmed cap, holding a Yankees banner.

The sailors began to rush to their friend's aid.

Khan raised a forefinger and twisted it in the air.

White with fright, Bobby put both legs over the top of the fence. The wind whipped at his peajacket and flat cap.

The crowd was pleading with him to come down, shouting for others to go for help.

Khan's fist tightened into a white-knuckled lump of muscle, tendon, and bone.

"Bobby!" his shipmates yelled.

Khan understood that it was going to have to be a forceful jump; that more than simply *ordering* him off the building, he was going to have to propel him clear of the structure's numerous ledges and setbacks as well.

As the first of the sailors reached the wall and began to climb to the rescue, Khan opened his hand, splaying tapering fingers—

And the sailor leapt like a frog into the howling

wind, a blood-curdling scream tearing from his throat as he plunged. Screams rose from the tourists on the observation deck in eerie response. People buried their faces in their hands, or in the shoulders of those nearby.

Only the preteen with the baseball banner took note of the motionless academic in the tweed jacket and the slightly grinning Chinese with a hand cupped to his ear, singing, "Come on along and listen to, the lullaby of Broadway ..."

16 Survival Lessons

The morning edition of *The Standard* had devoted space to the theft of a massive silver coffin from the Museum of Art and Antiquity, and a report that the police were investigating possible links between the recent deaths of a museum security guard and a hackie who had crashed his cab into a fuel truck. No mention was made of the disappearance of Dr. Reinhardt Lane, the deaths of the Marine sentries, or the bodies of five Asians found on the scene. Obviously the FBI was sitting tight on the story. Although—thanks to The Shadow's agent, Clyde Burke—a small article on page six of *The Classic* mentioned a stabbing in a Chinatown restaurant that had left one man dead.

"Shiwan Khan still needs one component to complete the bomb," Cranston was explaining to Margo as they hurried through Times Square toward the sanctum. He was wearing his customary black overcoat and homburg; Margo, "Aunt Rose's" black cashmere coat, whose layered collar was adorned with pieces of jaguar pelt; a modified cloche, also trimmed with pelt; black pumps; black suede gloves; and tortoiseshell sunglasses.

"He imported the radioactive fuel from China," Cranston went on. "The awesome potential of that substance can only be released by the intense pressure of an implosion lens—which is why he needs your father. But in order to initiate the reaction and contain the device up until the moment of detonation, he needs a supply of beryllium and polonium—"

"Farley Claymore," Margo said. She had stopped in the middle of the sidewalk, causing a chain reaction of collisions among other scurrying pedestrians. "My father's smarmy partner. He's been trying to convince me to look at some kind of sphere he's developed, and I'm sure he said it was made of beryllium."

Cranston's expression hardened. An implosion device and a beryllium sphere: benign inventions when taken singly, those brainstorms were being combined into a fearsome device. "Is the sphere in the Federal Building?"

Margo shook her head. "Farley's been running underwater tests on the thing downtown. At Mari-Tech Labs. It's on the lower West Side, near the Battery."

"Good, very good," Cranston said through gritted teeth.

Margo beamed at him. "See, I told you we had a connection."

He nearly smiled. "Listen, I need your help on something. There's a vacant lot at one-fifty-eight Second Avenue, where Second intersects Houston. It's probably the former site of a mansion or something. But I need to know what that something was."

"Sure. But why?"

"When I was chasing Khan last night, he gave me the slip in that area. And there was something about that lot . . ." He snapped out of it. "You'll need help running a background check, so I'm going to put you in touch with some people who assist me from time to time—a man named Harry Vincent, and another named Rutledge Mann. I'll instruct them to rendezvous with you at the city assessor's office in City Hall. Can you find your way there?"

Margo was nodding, trying to keep everything straight. "But what about Farley?"

Cranston's grin was anything but playful. "Mr. Claymore is going to receive a surprise visit from The Shadow."

Mari-Tech Labs comprised a cluster of buildings spread along the Hudson River, near the western terminus of Canal Street. Prominent among them was a spherical structure approximately two stories high, inside of which electronic components were tested for watertightness. Constructed of rib-reinforced aluminum alloy, the sphere was banded at the top by a catwalk that was accessed by a curving, metal stairway. Given its porthole and spoked wheel, the sphere's single doorway most resembled a submarine hatch.

The catwalk had become Claymore's favorite haunt when he wasn't busy supervising submersion tests on the beryllium sphere. Just now, he was pacing the walk, clucking and giggling to himself, his puffy eyes searching the horizon, as if for a long overdue storm. The January air smelled of the river. Close by, two tugboats were tied up at Mari-Tech's pier.

"Scoff at Farley Claymore, will they?" he muttered. "Not for much longer. Not when they see what I've created, and what I'm about to become." He wrapped his arms about himself. "Now you'll come around, Margo Lane. You and all the rest who've spurned me." He gave a downward tug to the sleeves of his camel-hair overcoat.

How his life had changed since the aeolian harp had been delivered to his apartment. A misrouted package, a gift from a secret admirer ... he had never learned who sent the thing. But it wasn't New York's winter wind that had played the instrument's strings, but a distant wind from China—one that had spoken to him, informing him of his true identity and of the identity of the master he served. Not Reinhardt Lane, that was for certain. And not the government of the United States, either. In fact, an altogether different war department.

He chortled to himself and was about to resume his pacing when he heard a squeaking sound from below. Leaning over the catwalk's pipe railing, he saw the hatch closing of its own accord.

Well, well, he thought. An intruder.

Claymore hurried down the staircase and rushed through the hatch. He couldn't have been more than a minute behind his uninvited guest, but the domed, seamlessly sealed chamber appeared to be empty. That in itself was curious, since the sphere didn't afford many places of concealment. Claymore's eyes scanned the interior, nevertheless. It was, however, his ears that were offered the first clue.

"Farley Claymore," intoned a sibilant, menacing voice that seemed to originate from all directions.

Claymore reacted as one might expect: he started and whirled. "Who's there?"

Instead of answering, the intruder posed an unexpected question. "The beryllium sphere, Claymore. Where is it?"

"Sphere?" Claymore asked, still turning in circles.

"What sphere? I don't know what you're talking about—whoever you are." He scurried about the circular chamber in what seemed to be agitation, searching for the source of the voice. "Come out and show yourself."

A taunting, contemptuous laugh answered him. "All in due time, Claymore. But first tell me how and when you fell under the spell of Shiwan Khan."

Claymore stiffened. "I've never heard that name."

"Claymore, you fool," the voice barked. "You're being manipulated. Your mind is being controlled through the power of remote hypnosis."

With hidden purpose, Claymore began to sway on his feet. "My mind—controlled?"

The voice grew impatient. "The sphere. What have you done with it?"

"I—It's not here. Someone took it away."

The Shadow imitated Claymore's ordinarily unctuous tone. "Take me to it—now!"

Claymore seemed paralyzed; then he shrieked with laughter. "Not likely!" He rushed to a series of control levers that protruded from the curved wall, and he threw one of them. A few feet above the floor, two diametrically opposed intake valves opened, admitting a violent surge of water.

"*No one* controls my mind, Shadow," Claymore called out, as water spewed across the floor of the sphere. "I'm honored to work for my Khan. A new world order is on the horizon, and in it I'm going to rule as a king! Do you hear me—a king!" He whipped a revolver from his jacket pocket and aimed it toward the center of the room.

The Shadow laughed derisively. "And just who are you planning to shoot with that, Claymore?"

Claymore traversed the weapon. The water was already several inches deep and rising rapidly, running evenly across the floor—except for a certain area, where it swirled in two small eddies, each about a foot long.

Claymore grinned. "Khan told me you were arrogant, Shadow. Now it's going to cost you!"

With a chilling laugh that mimicked The Shadow's own, Claymore emptied the gun in the direction of the eddies—where two feet might be positioned. No taunts answered him this time; only the sound of rushing water. He squinted at a distant portion of wall, where the revolver's rounds had left a row of evenly spaced holes, one every eighteen inches or so—save for between the third and fourth holes, where the hull of the sphere was intact for almost a yard.

Claymore lowered his eyes to the surging water below the target area. As he watched, drops of blood falling from thin air swirled in the water, staining it pink.

Claymore's laugh was triumphant. He swung to the control panel and threw the remaining levers, opening additional intake valves high overhead. Foaming water gushed into the sphere from all sides.

"I may be back in a short while, Shadow," Claymore announced as he was locking the levers. "But don't hold your breath!"

Soaked to his knees, he moved to the hatch, then disappeared through it, bracing the wheel behind him, his exit punctuated by peals of deranged laughter.

Lying waterlogged and gunshot in rapidly rising water, The Shadow heard Claymore's feet on the stairway leading from the hatch, then the sound of a truck, starting and accelerating toward Mari-Tech's front gate. One of Claymore's carefully placed shots had caught him in the left shoulder. But this was no arrow wound; the round was still inside him and he was bleeding profusely, enough to have already saturated part of the cloak.

Clutching his shoulder, he dragged himself to his feet and staggered through thigh-deep water to the control panel, knowing full well that Claymore had locked the levers but tugging on them just the same. He tried the wheel of the hatch, as well; even slammed his hand repeatedly against the thick glass of the porthole, all to no avail.

Weakened by blood loss, he sagged against the door, blacking out for a few moments. When his eyes blinked open, the water was at waist level and still rising.

The sphere was going to become his tomb if he didn't do something soon.

He closed his eyes and thought of Margo.

"I need you," he said weakly, and slumped against the hatch.

The water continued to fountain from the valves and billow around him, rising to his chest; then, his neck. Its faintly briny smell woke him with a start. With effort, he pulled off his hat and shrugged out of the cloak, becoming Lamont Cranston now: vulnerable, plainly visible, and trapped.

He kicked his feet and paddled with his uninjured arm, keeping himself afloat as the chamber filled. For a while he was able to float on his back and conserve his strength. But as the water rose toward the sphere's flat circle of ceiling, there was no room for floating. At some point he dove for the hatch again and attempted to turn the wheel, thinking that perhaps the pressure of the water had loosened it.

It didn't budge.

And by the time he regained the surface, there was little more than six inches of air between the water level and ceiling. He had to throw his head back and crane his neck to snag a breath of air.

The distance dwindled to four inches of space.

Then two inches.

Barely enough to accommodate his hawklike nose.

17 Messages Sent on the Wind

Swallowing and wallowing and reswallowing gulps of deoxygenated air, Cranston felt as if he were about to implode. His shoulder wound had ceased to be a concern. Three minutes earlier he had managed a final nasal inhalation, but now the sphere was completely filled with water. Born of his desperate struggles to set a new record for breath-holding, however, had come an idea.

Submerged five feet above the floor, he began inspecting the neat row of bullet holes Farley Claymore's revolver had punched in the aluminum-alloy wall. His forefinger probed each of the holes, searching for the one of largest diameter. When he discovered the one best suited to his purpose, he plugged it with his finger for a moment; then removed his finger to observe the action of the water as it reentered the hole. That action told him that Claymore's shot had penetrated the wall.

A mere inch away was oxygen in abundance.

Cranston pressed his mouth to the hole, summoning the last of his air in a forced exhale to expel particles from the opening; then, with his mouth suctioned to the smooth wall, he inhaled slowly.

During his apprenticeship with Marpa Tulku, much attention had been given to breath control, and that training served Cranston well as he continued to nurse the bullet hole, wondering all the while just how long he could hold out.

Margo slid her maroon La Salle coupe to a halt in front of Mari-Tech's test facility and raced from the driver's seat to the structure's recessed, round-topped hatch. Despite her coming closer and closer to him, The Shadow's voice had been growing weaker the past few minutes. Her instincts told her that he was in grave danger.

She had been in City Hall, in the assessor's office, when she had perceived The Shadow's remote call for help.

As promised, his agents had rendezvoused with her there—the portly Rutledge Mann, and the handsome Harry Vincent, who had immediately tried to sweet-talk her—but neither of them had come up with any information on the vacant lot that had become something of an idée fixe with Cranston. Strangely, information on recent activities at 158 Second Avenue was missing from the primary records, and her only option had been to sort through the office's backup records, which comprised stacks and stacks of blueprints and property documents waiting to be filed.

Luck had been with her, though, because she had managed to locate a promising file. She was hunched over a table spread with blueprints and ledgers when the force of The Shadow's entreaty had thrown her backward into her chair, eliciting looks of concern from several office staffers seated at desks and standing at nearby file drawers.

The only experience she could compare it to was a time she had fallen off a swing as a child and had had the wind knocked out of her. Her first thought was that she was suffering an allergic reaction to the dusty shelves of the file room or to the stacks of yellowing paper. But with the joyous return of her breath came the clear sound of Cranston's voice: not in the room, but inside her head, not unlike the soundless voice she used when she talked to herself, but more lucid, present.

I need you, the voice said. . . .

That had been twenty minutes earlier—the time it had taken to hurry from City Hall and to bend a number of traffic rules during the short drive to Mari-Tech.

Water was leaking around the edges of the hatch that accessed the sphere, as if some experiment was in progress. Could The Shadow be elsewhere? she asked herself. Had she somehow gotten her telepathic signals crossed? She was about to press her face to the brass-rimmed observation window that dimpled the hatch when Cranston's own bobbed into view, his deformed features a clear indication that he was near drowning.

Ignoring the soaking she was taking, she began to tug on the door handle until she realized that the hatch was secured by a wheel, which itself was locked by a heavy bar with a T-handle. Extricating the bar from the spokes, she put her hands on the wheel and gave it a counterclockwise twist. It hadn't gone a half turn when the hatch burst open, disgorging a raging cascade of water. Her hands fastened on the staircase's pipe railing, but the torrent proved too much for her, engulfing and sweeping her face first down the stairs. Only moments behind came Cranston, rolling and tumbling onto the parking apron that fronted the sphere.

Drenched to the bone and coughing water, Margo sat up in the river's delta. Remarkably, her hat was still on—though hardly at the same rakish angle—but the cashmere coat and black satin dress would never be the same. She spied Cranston's inert form faceup in newly created mud a few feet away. Getting to her feet, she rushed to him, petrified that she hadn't arrived in time to save him.

He coughed and regurgitated an enormous amount of water. But at least he was breathing. When she leaned over him and touched his face, his eyes opened, then blinked, fighting for focus.

"You called," she said, cradling his head.

He showed her a weak smile. "You heard."

Shiwan Khan's imperial guard, greatly reduced in number, paid salute to their ruler, the sound of their triumphant hissing filling the throne room. Quickly sated on their praise, Khan silenced them with a raised finger.

"Yes, we are victorious. And, as victors, we are entitled to reap the spoils of war." He gazed down at them. "Trust that I will remember each and every one of you."

Khan stepped down off the throne to approach Farley Claymore, who stood proudly in the sunken center of the room, his creation resting beside him on a four-wheeled wagon with a long handle: an orb of burnished metal that shone like monel, three feet in diameter—Claymore's beryllium sphere.

"Especially remembered will be my foreign agent," Khan said, coming to Claymore's side. "The only American possessed of sufficient intelligence to recognize my genius and to join me of his . . . own free will."

Claymore shone as brightly as the silvery sphere. He used his handkerchief to polish a blemish from the orb's reflective surface.

Khan regarded him for a moment, then gave the back of Claymore's neck what began as an affectionate squeeze. "My loyal subject," he said, tightening his grip, "who fancies himself a king in *my* kingdom."

Claymore's grin collapsed. "King?" he said in sudden alarm. "Did I say 'king'? What was I thinking? Confronted with The Shadow, one tends to reach for words—"

Khan brought his left hand to Claymore's face and squeezed, as if to crush his skull. "Indeed." He twisted Claymore's head to one side, impeding his breathing, then spun him in a circle.

"Actually, I was thinking prince—tops," Claymore managed fulsomely. "Though I'd be more than happy with duke. Or baron. Whatever suits my Khan. The choice of title is of little consequence. I am honored simply to serve—"

Khan withdrew his hands, but held out a finger in warning. "Retrieve Dr. Lane and begin assembly of the bomb." He moved to the stairs below his throne and spread his arms over the sphere. "Alert the press," he told his guard. "The new order is at hand. Submit or perish. In the name of the new Kha Khan, Ruler of the Dwellers of all Cities, Emperor of Humankind, the Power of God on Earth!"

The five Mongols drew their sabers, raising some, lowering others, to form the sacred character of conquest.

The round that had found The Shadow had passed almost completely though his shoulder without striking bone. But the wound was serious, nonetheless. By evening an infection had taken root, and he was running a high fever, drifting in and out of delirium.

Even so, Cranston had refused to send for a doctor. Removing the bullet and dressing the wound had been left to Margo, whose mother—a volunteer during the war—had taught her just enough first aid to meet Cranston's needs. Too, the Shadow kept what amounted to a hospital medicine cabinet in the house, the reason for which Margo understood when she saw him with his shirt off: the man had more scar tissue than undamaged flesh. Under a bandage he had applied to his right shoulder only two nights earlier was a gash from an arrow.

It was the middle of the night, and Margo, wearing Cranston's brown-and-gold-patterned silk robe, was in the upstairs hallway, returning to his room with a glass bowl of cool water when she heard him moan in anguish. Clenched hands to his chest, face beaded with sweat, he was tossing and turning when she entered the room and moved to the edge of the bed to comfort him. She dipped a cloth into the bowl and began to mop his brow. Leaning toward him she thought he was awake but soon realized that he was dreaming with his eyes open!

Looking into someone's eyes without that person being aware of you was like looking into the eyes of a blind person, and Margo didn't like it one bit. Still, she felt drawn to his unfocused gaze, which seemed lit from within, by flames that flickered deep in his soul. Drawn, mothlike to those flames; so much so that she seemed to leave her own body and plunge into the fiery heart of him—

Suddenly finding herself standing by a fireplace in

the dank confines of a stone castle. Light from the fire illuminated the back of a thronelike chair on the far side of the room, and in it, the figure of man, whose right hand rested on the chair's elaborately carved arm. Over the knuckles of that hand rolled a seed capsule of some sort, in a way that brought to Margo's mind an image of Lamont Cranston on the night they met, manipulating a coin with his fingers.

She wanted a closer look at the seated figure, and to her astonishment, she found that she could actually navigate this dreamscape. Like some wraith floating on the drafts of the castle, she approached the chair and began to edge around it. Cranston himself was slouched there, long-haired and unwashed, though dressed in richly detailed black silk. And once more a memory surfaced in Margo's mind: of the entranced few minutes she had spent in the company of Shiwan Khan.

Cranston seemed to be aware of her presence. His filthy hand gripped the seed capsule, and he looked up at her sharply, his empty eyes underscored by the dark circles of addiction.

"Who invited you here?" he asked her.

A log shifted in the fireplace, and Margo whirled toward it. She seemed to merge with the fire, its flames engulfing everything. But in them, as sometimes happened in clouds, images took shape: of a battlefield strewn with bloodied corpses; of hordes of soldiers on horseback racing down a mountainside; of Cranston himself, saber in hand, face streaked with blood and dirt, voicing a battle cry—

The cry seemed to become her own as she recoiled from the violence of his mind, retreating to the safe harbor of her own body, in his bedroom, her gaze still fixed on the flames in his eyes, but her mind cut off from the rage and brutality of his former life.

Cranston awakened and, with some effort, sat up, dazed.

"You were dreaming," she whispered.

He thought for a moment, staring at her. "You saw?"

When she nodded, he turned away from her.

"I've done things I can never forgive myself for," he said weakly.

She tried to quiet his distress. "Whoever you were, whatever you did, it's in the past."

He shook his head. "Not for me, Margo. Never for me."

She leaned her face to his, and their lips met in a languid kiss.

18 The Gathering Storm

A slow news week, the papers were unusually attentive to Khan's issued threats. The banner headline of *The New York Daily World-Telegram* read: MADMAN THREATENS TO BLOW CITY SKY-HIGH WITH ATOMIC DEVICE, DEMANDS BILLIONS IN RANSOM! And beneath that: WARNS PRESIDENT: "JOIN ME OR PERISH."

Street corner newsboys gave voice to the front page, doling out papers by the stackful to panicked crowds of pedestrians. Families gathered round their radios, eager for news updates. By telegraph, teletype, telephone, and shortwave, word of Khan's "New Order" spread round the world.

In the mansion drawing room, Cranston crunched the front page of the *World-Telegram* into a ball and pitched it across the room. The press was having a field day with the story, apparently indifferent to the fact that Khan had already been implicated in at least one kidnapping and as many as five deaths—the museum guard, an innocent cabbie, the two Marine sentries, and a sailor who may have inadvertently insulted him at the Empire State Building. But only *The Classic* was playing up those angles—and then only because of efforts by The Shadow's agents.

"Khan is demanding priceless works of art, precious

gems, even silks," Margo was saying, after bringing the papers to Cranston's attention. "He's demanding that everything be delivered by midnight, the start of the Chinese New Year."

Cranston gently massaged his wounded shoulder. He was dressed in a white shirt and high-waisted black trousers supported by braces. Margo was wearing his robe and was barefoot.

Scowling, Cranston turned away from the room's wall of tall Palladium windows. "Funds to finance renovations of Xanadu, no doubt," he muttered.

A butler appeared with coffee. Cranston and Margo rendezvoused with him in the center of the room.

"The government is refusing to cede to his demands," Margo went on. "The Secretary of Defense claims that an atom bomb can't be built."

The butler served the coffee, handing Cranston a cup. "They don't want to admit that they've been beaten to the punch," he said. "Find Khan, and we'll find the bomb." He cut his eyes to Margo. "Did you learn anything about that vacant lot?"

Margo compressed her lips and took the cup from his hand before he had a chance to sip. "Not much, I'm afraid. It was the site of the Hotel Monolith. The building was almost completed seven years ago—wine cellar, furnishings, ballroom, the works—but it never opened. The owner went bankrupt in the Crash and committed suicide, and the building had to be sold."

Cranston considered it. "The Monolith. I remember it. Twelve stories tall, very Moderne. A top-floor club or something . . ."

"It seems like that's all that *anybody* can remember about it. The property was purchased by an Asian buyer five years ago, but the buyer and the city couldn't come to terms about the height of the hotel in relation to the width of the street, or some damn thing, and the building was torn down."

Cranston frowned. "What year was that?"

Margo shook her head. "I know this sounds strange, but I haven't been able to find out. I made a few calls to the newspapers and such, but all anybody remembers is the suicide and the sale—nothing about the actual demolition. Everyone seems to know it was torn down, but not when or by whom."

Cranston snatched the cup back and took a sip. "Or *if*."

Two hours later, Cranston and Margo were standing across the street from the lot itself, and he was regarding it with stunned disbelief.

"He actually did it," Cranston said, more to himself. "He has mastered Marpa Tulku's greatest feat."

Margo eyed the trash-filled, fenced-in lot dubiously. "He who—Shiwan Khan?" Turning toward Cranston, she realized that he was deep in concentration. His eyes were narrowed, his face was rigid, and the veins in his neck were bulging slightly. "Lamont!" she said, hoping to pull him out of it.

But her distress wasn't registering. Or if it was, she saw no evidence of it. As she watched, the veins in his forehead began to distend and throb; in fact, his entire head seemed to be quivering.

They had stopped by her apartment on their way downtown, where she'd changed into a blue satin dress, its cuffs and V-neckline accented with velvet ribbon. Over that she wore a nubby wool coat, trimmed with black Persian lamb fur. Her hands were jammed into a black muff, and she wore a flat, black hat, tilted low over one eye. Shrevnitz, seated at the wheel of his hack, had supplied the transportation. Though some people were dismissing Khan's threats as those of a raving lunatic, the city was in an anxious mood, uncertain it would survive to see another day. Even Shrevvy, who had seen more oddities than most people, was plainly worried.

"Lamont, please," Margo tried again. Cranston's features, nose and eyebrows especially, were undergoing a change. She was about to take hold of him and shake him out of it when on his own he emerged from the trance.

"Good god, it's beautiful," he said.

Margo followed his rapt gaze but saw nothing but the lot, auto and pedestrian traffic hurrying past it. "What's beautiful?"

Finally he acknowledged her. "The Hotel Monolith. It's there, still standing! He has somehow hypnotized the entire city into believing that it was torn down, and cloaked it from sight." He laughed wickedly. "The ways of the master mind are many and devious, and the clouded mind sees *nothing*!"

Margo stared at him in transparent concern. He was taking on that familiar look, that look she'd seen outside the Cobalt Club and in the bedroom of the mansion. As if there was something frightful building inside him. Only more so, now. His profile appeared almost hawkish; his eyes had become sharp orbs of burning, blue power.

"But *I* see," he said, sneering. "He can't hide from me."

Margo glanced at the lot. "See what, Lamont? Shiwan Khan? Is that who you see? Talk to me, Lamont!"

He looked right through her, denying her any actuality or presence. "You and Shrevnitz will soon receive instructions. Follow them precisely." He whirled and went to the cab, opening the rear door and taking something from a compartment under the seat.

"Lamont," she said, hurrying after him, "if you know where Khan is, we can get help."

His only response was to slam the door and start off down the street, a parcel of black fabric tucked under his good arm. Margo cut her eyes to Shrevnitz, but he looked away, refusing to meet her gaze. Then she turned and followed Cranston, keeping a safe distance.

"You don't have to do this alone," she called after him. "It doesn't have to be this way."

Cranston hastened his pace, hurrying past a tavern, a haberdasher's, a cleaning and dyeing shop. The day, which had begun overcast, was growing steadily darker, colder, and windier. A storm seemed imminent.

Cranston made a sudden turn into a dark alley. Margo pursued him. With the gloomy sky and closeness of the opposing brick walls, it may as well have been twilight.

Up ahead, Cranston had stopped. Margo watched silently as he pulled a wide-brimmed hat from the folds of his parcel and slipped it on, tugging it down over his forehead.

"Lamont, this isn't who you are!" she said, aching for him.

Forked lightning split the sky overhead, brighter than a photographer's flash, and ear-splitting thunder rumbled in the alley. Cranston raised his face enough for her to see into his eyes.

"A conjured storm to frighten the fainthearted," he said in that same contemptuous tone. "A magician's parlor trick."

And all at once Lamont Cranston was gone.

In his place, caparisoned in palpable blackness, stood The Shadow, a red scarf covering his mouth and chin, his long cloak rippling and billowing in the drafts.

"This is who I am," he told Margo with an icy laugh.

She reeled back against the wall as he moved away from her into the day's thickening darkness, a drop of ink dissolving into a blotter, his trailing laugh resounding over the strident sound of the wind and the peal of ominous thunder.

In the throne room, Reinhardt Lane's implosion orb—now armed with individually sequestered bronzium bullets—hung suspended in Farley Claymore's beryllium sphere. Lane, compliant and oblivious to all distractions, had his hands thrust deep into the sphere, working furiously to complete the wiring of the initiator and the shaped detonation charges.

Claymore stood over him, hectoring him. "Bet you wish you'd been nicer to me now, Professor. Bet you wish you'd listened to *my* idea for a change. Didn't count on me being tight with a conqueror, did you?"

"That's quite enough," Khan ordered, much to the disappointment of the remaining members of the imperial guard.

Claymore gagged himself. Lane was finished anyway, and Claymore was finished with him.

Khan descended from his throne to appraise the completed device. "Activate the bomb," he said when Lane had closed and secured the sphere's quarter-section access lid. "These fool Americans dare to doubt me. Soon they will witness my wrath."

Claymore had fitted a timer into the face of the sphere. The display consisted of five Nixie tubes behind a rectangular curved-glass panel a foot long. Each vacuum tube contained a complement of ten filament numerals that glowed red during activation. The timer mechanism itself was accessed by a second panel of equal size, located adjacent to and just below the display.

The timer had been preset to count down from two hours, zero minutes, zero seconds.

Khan caressed the sphere's silvery surface as the seconds began to flash by. "You are certain you can fashion others as I require them?" he asked Claymore.

Claymore nodded with enthusiasm. "It's a cinch."

Khan glanced at Lane. "That renders Professor Lane redundant." He looked to his guards. "Secure him in one of the rooms. His own invention will be the death of him."

Lane reacted to the mention of his name. "That's nice, dear," he said blankly.

A delighted Claymore watched one of the guards lead Lane from the circular room. He waited until the pair had exited before sidling up to Shiwan Khan. "I know you must have this covered, but shouldn't *we* be finalizing plans to leave the city?"

Khan regarded him with distaste. "A flying machine is waiting to take us to safety. We depart in one hour."

Claymore fell silent for a long moment, vaguely disturbed by Khan's choice of words. "Uh, you do mean a *plane*, don't you?"

19 The Powers of the Unseen

Burbank, ever-viligant dispatcher of pneumatic tube canisters and encrypted mail, sat in his swivel chair in the dimly lighted control nexus of The Shadow's clandestine network. It happened to be past sundown, but Burbank never paid much attention to the hour; his biological clock ran according to no known human pattern. His jacket was draped over the back of the chair, and the radio headset was snugged to his ears. The huddle of brass-banded canisters on his desk and the forest of colored pins in the city map on the wall gave some indication of how busy he had been since Shiwan Khan's arrival in New York.

But The Shadow had not been idle, either.

"Understood," Burbank murmured into his microphone, in acknowledgment of the crimefighter's latest communiqué.

He shut off the radio and dispatched two canisters in quick succession. Then he reached for two sheets of stationery and a fountain pen. There was nothing remarkable about the pen; the ink, however, was a variation of the type the French counterespionage service called *encre sympathique*—invisible ink. As for the creamy sheets of stationery, they were impregnated with a substance that reacted to the time-release ink. So while

Burbank's thin hand moved deftly across the page, the pen strokes wouldn't appear until much later.

Finished with the first note, he used a signet ring moistened with that same ink to append The Shadow's silhouette to the bottom on the page. Immediately he set to work on the second. In the end, both meticulously folded notes were inserted into unmarked envelopes.

He rose from his seat and donned his jacket and overcoat. On his way out of the subterranean crypt, he retrieved from its tall stand an umbrella with a Prince of Wales handle.

The two letters were in one hand when he emerged on the street, the opened umbrella in the other. A violent rainstorm had caught the city by surprise and the sidewalks were crowded with other umbrella wielders. Tip to tip, the dozens of umbrellas per block had created a kind of nomadic tarpaulin.

The nondescript Burbank maneuvered through the throng with professional ease. Then, at a certain corner, he paused and, in defiance of the downpour, closed the umbrella. Gripping it under his right arm, he took one of the letters in his right hand and stepped from the curb directly into the eastbound traffic lane. The letter hand was extended slightly behind him when a bicycle messenger sped by and snatched the letter.

Undeterred by the fountaining wake launched by the bike's thick tires, Burbank walked on, extending the letter in his left hand slightly in front of him as he entered the westbound traffic lane, where a second bicycle messenger, headed in the opposite direction, grabbed hold of it as he whisked by.

Anyone observing him at just that moment might have noticed a hint of a satisfied smile assemble itself on his narrow face. But in short order the umbrella opened, and Burbank was swallowed by the crowd.

Moe Shrevnitz and his wife were listening to the sound of the rain lashing against the windows of their Brooklyn flat when one of the envelopes appeared from under the front door, as if propelled by the wind. Shrevnitz, lounging in his form-fitting armchair by the fire, noticed it and hurried to the door. The suddenness of his action made Shirl look up from her knitting.

"What is it, Moe?" she asked while he was tearing into the envelope. "Another flyer from the bowling league?"

She was a plain-looking woman, who had put on as many pounds as he had over the long years of their uneventful marriage. She did, however, have a suspicious streak Shrevnitz had never been able to extinguish—one that made for problems when he was called on to do The Shadow's bidding.

"Moe?" Shirl repeated. "What is it?"

Shrevnitz's eyes were riveted to the page. Quickened by exposure to air, the time-release ink was bringing Burbank's short message to light. *Shrevnitz*, it read, *Meet at northeast corner Houston and Second, headquarters Shiwan Khan.*

"Moe!" Shirl said.

He glanced at her, then stepped out of sight to the hall closet. "Uh, yeah, it's from the league all right. They want me to fill in for somebody at the lanes."

"On a night like tonight?" she called.

"I know, I know, but what's a guy to do?"

When he reappeared in the parlor he was wearing his peacoat and had his red-cloth bowling bag dangling from one hand. He tossed the crumpled letter into the fire.

"After the game, we might go out for a beer or something. You know how it is. If all the guys are going, I can't really say no, so . . ." He planted a kiss on her furrowed forehead. "I guess you shouldn't wait up."

He tugged his cap on and hurried for the front door.

But no sooner did the door close than Shirl was up and out of her chair, the knitting set aside, and rushing for the hearth's wrought-iron poker. The note was already burning at the edges, but she managed to fish it free of the flames before too much damage had been done. By then, however, Burbank's near calligraphic script was fading, and Shirl found herself staring at a blank page.

Across the East River, in a brownstone in the heart of the city, the ink was fading fast from the second of Burbank's notes. Alongside the note on the antique table was a candlestick telephone, an unfinished cup of coffee, and a still-burning cigarette that bore traces of bright red lipstick.

Margo regarded the letter and envelope as she shrugged into her nubby wool coat. When they stood at the site of the apparently psychically cloaked Hotel Monolith, Cranston had said she would receive instructions, and so she had. Having seen him in his guise as The Shadow, however—having glimpsed his true face—she was more apprehensive than eager about allying herself with him. For her father's sake, yes, she would do what Cranston said. But she was suddenly frightened of him, almost as frightened as she was of Shiwan Khan, The Shadow's shadow.

* * *

Hulagu and Shu Shiang stood guard on either side of the central pair of front doors to the building the Kha Khan affirmed was invisible to the city and its millions of inhabitants. There were six doors in all, gleaming white, sandwiched between blue-glaze tiled columns that striped the facade of the twelve-story hotel. Shiwan Khan had conjured a monsoon-strength storm for New York's final day, but the Mongol bowmen would gladly have endured more than a wind-lashed drenching in service to their lord and master.

Hulagu, however, was growing increasingly uneasy about a distant squishing sound his ears had seized on and refused to surrender. Uneasy, because Shu Shiang either didn't hear the sound over the angry thrumming of the rain or wouldn't say—even when the sound had increased in volume and frequency, as if on the approach.

Perhaps his partner's peaked helmet was too tight a fit, Hulagu told himself.

He had his mouth open to say as much when he saw Shu Shiang blanch and point to something in front of him—a splashing in the muddy lake the rain had fashioned in the tapering trapezoid of marble that fronted the building. The veiled source of the sound was very close now, and Hulagu watched in nervous astonishment as footprints began to appear in the mud near the hotel's gilded, inlaid monogram. It was as if someone was charging for the front doors, only *there wasn't anyone there.*

Neither bowman had forgotten their encounter with Ying Ko in the scientist's laboratory, but so rapid was the stride of The Shadow that they scarcely had time to raise their weapons in defense. Blackness darker than night clouded the space before Hulagu's eyes, and his face took a sudden, ferocious pounding. His high cheekbones were shattered, his lips smashed, his ribs cracked. . . . A few moments of this, and unconsciousness seemed infinitely preferable—even if it did entail a face-first collapse into the mud.

Enthroned on the hotel's top floor—in what was originally planned to have been the Moonlight Café—Shiwan Khan surfaced from contemplation as the sound of his arch-rival's mocking laugh reached him. "Ying Ko," he seethed.

Hugging himself in naked alarm, Farley Claymore spun around to face the throne. "The Shadow?" His eyes searched the room. "Where? Here?"

Khan shot him a withering glance. "Not here, you fool. But, yes, inside the building. In the lobby."

Claymore gulped and found his voice. "Can you tell from here if he's mad at me? I think he might be. We had a little misunderstanding yesterday, and I think there might be some hard feelings—"

"Find him and kill him," Khan barked.

Claymore motioned to himself. "Me? Kill him?"

Khan turned to the three remaining warriors of his guard. The bald Hoang Shu was cradling a Thompson. "All of you, find him and kill him."

Claymore lowered his head. "If it's all the same with you, I'd just as soon stay here and help—"

"Do as I say!" Khan said, shooting to his feet. He came down the carpeted stairs, snatched the tommy from Hoang's grip, and forced it on Claymore. "This may help. Now, go."

Claymore gazed at the gun in mute disbelief. He was about to protest when two of the Mongols took hold of him and hustled him from the room. Khan settled back into the throne, arranging himself in a regal posture.

The sphere was suspended from a single cable, five feet above the broad circle of sunken floor. The vacuum tubes of the timer showed one hour, twenty-six minutes, fourteen seconds.

And counting.

"Plenty of time," the descendant of conquerors assured himself. "I wouldn't miss this, even for the world."

"A flashlight?" Claymore was saying to one of the guards a few minutes later. He was winded from the walk down from the twelfth floor and anxious to avoid a second encounter with The Shadow. The tommy gun shook in his hands. "You're planning to give him what for with a *flashlight*?"

The helmeted Mongol glanced at him in angry incomprehension and continued to play his light across the walls, ceiling, and floor of the carpeted hallway. Ornate sconces threw just enough light to see by. Ahead of them the corridor ended in a T-intersection, with the baroque hotel lobby off to the right, down a center-banistered staircase—a study in Modernist Parisian excess, with arching columns, gaudy cornices, and balustraded balconies. Hoang Shu, his curved saber raised in front of him, had the point position.

Still eyeing the flashlight when they arrived at the landing, Claymore smiled in sudden realization. "Now I see. You're going to try to catch him in the beam." He laughed nervously and wagged a finger. "Very, very clever. Though wait till I tell you about how I trapped him at Mari-Tech—"

A laugh—a macabre phrase of shuddering ridicule—floated up from somewhere in the lobby. The three Mongols traded looks of sudden apprehension. Claymore wrenched the flashlight away from the bowman.

"You men check the lobby," he said, already hurrying off in the opposite direction.

Easily commanded, even by someone as spineless as Farley Claymore, the guards obeyed, though reluctantly. The Shadow's jeering laugh came at intervals, beckoning them down into the hotel's vast kitchen, and beyond that into a fully stocked wine cellar.

With bracing intakes of breath, the trio edged into the dark room, curved blades and hair-trigger crossbows at the ready. Hoang Shu clicked instructions, and they spread out to search the several aisles, stopping occasionally to exchange updates in that same tongue-clicking code.

The Shadow's slow cackle, echoing through the cool cellar, was at once chilling and challenging.

Misgiving wrinkling his glabrous scalp, Hoang Shu crept between rows of tall, wooden racks; at a junction of two narrow aisles, he stopped to peer carefully around the corner, his blade in hand. Darkness met his gaze, and into it he began to move—only to hear the snap of The Shadow's cloak and to feel the force of his gloved and ringed fist. Hoang's hands flew involuntarily to his flattened nose, but even they were no safeguard against the power of The Shadow's second and third blows. With each, the broken nasal bones were driven further into the Mongol's skull. Hoang's tongue clicked once, as if in farewell, and he crumpled to the floor.

Elsewhere in the cellar, the muffled sounds of Hoang's pummeling were not lost on the other two Mongols, who were crawling down separate aisles a couple of rows apart, trembling, leather-fletched bolts nocked in their crossbows. Reaching the ends of their respective aisles at the same moment, each stopped to listen, completely unaware of the other's presence.

Just then, however, an ink-black slithering seemed to debouch from the aisle that separated them, dislodging two wine bottles in its swift passing. The bottles hit the floor and shattered, bringing each bowman around, firing blindly toward the sound, their short-shafted quarrels traversing the short distance in a split-second, straight into each other's chests.

Waving the flashlight about, Claymore came rushing through double doors into an immense, empty space. High above him, strewn with chandeliers, arched an expanse of wooden ceiling, covered end to end with recessed squares of decoratively trimmed panels. The ballroom, he told himself, taking a moment to catch his breath. He leaned over, putting his hands on his knees, the machine gun wedged under his right arm.

He knew, from an earlier reconnaissance of the building, that the double doors on the far side of the room opened on a corridor whose windows overlooked the lobby, and that off the corridor was a stairway that led down to the hotel's secondary entrance, on Houston Street. And that was where he wanted to be—outside. Far from The Shadow, from Shiwan Khan, from a city that was about to be atomized.

He had the flashlight trained on the exit doors and was hurrying toward them when they suddenly slammed shut. He knew better to believe the wind was responsible, howling though it was outside the ballroom's wall of heavily draped windows.

The Shadow's laugh filled the room.

A scream of mortal terror tore itself from Claymore's throat, and he gyrated through several circles, aiming the light this way and that to no effect. He was considering racing back the way he had come when those doors, too, slammed shut.

"Did you think you'd never hear from me again, Claymore?" The Shadow asked in a low tone.

Claymore swung the light in crazed arcs, ultimately catching sight of a shadow on the far wall—that of a hawk-faced man in a cloak and a tall, wide-brimmed hat. Claymore's right arm came up and the tommy spoke to the sinister silhouette, spewing casings and sending rounds tearing into the paneled wall.

"I'm right here," The Shadow announced in a voice that parodied Claymore's.

Claymore twirled, aimed the light at another shadow on the wall and the staccato crackling commenced once more.

"Right here, Claymore," the voice said from elsewhere.

A third shadow appeared, and the tommy barked.

"Here—all around you!"

A fourth shadow sprung up, then a fifth and a sixth, until Claymore was surrounded by dozens of hawkish silhouettes. Laughing madly, he rotated in place, his finger frozen on the trigger. Rounds ripped into the walls and wooden ceiling, blades of flame shooting from the jerking muzzle of the gun until it had depleted itself.

Claymore let the overheated weapon slip from his grasp, then followed it to the chevron-patterned floor, down on his hands and knees, blubbering in abject terror, The Shadow's savage laugh assaulting his ears. From the very start, that rising taunt had expressed who was in control.

"Coward," Claymore mumbled. "Yellow belly. Show yourself and fight like a man."

Close by, The Shadow cleared his throat.

Claymore whirled to the sound and found himself gazing up at a black tower, slashed with red. Eyes that burned like The Shadow's shouldn't have produced a frigid effect, but they did. Gurgling with fear, Claymore felt himself yanked off his feet by his shirtfront and lifted high over head.

"Why, Claymore," The Shadow said, in a tone of mocking disapproval, "you're . . . drooling."

Returned to the floor, the slavering Claymore was too strickened to speak. But not to laugh—insanely—or to act. With sudden strength only fear can muster, he scrambled to his feet and bounded across the room, hurling himself through the double doors that led to the corridor. In the wall opposite was a truncated pyramid of frosted glass, etched with the Monolith's monogram. Claymore stared at it, shrugging in abject defeat; then, with a desperateness born of madness, he hurled himself through it, plunging to his death in the lobby below.

The Shadow understood that Shiwan Khan would be drawn to the sanctity of high places: mountaintops in his native Mongolia, the tops of tall buildings here in the city.

The entrance to what was to have been the Monolith's roof-top dance club was accessed by a wide stairway, carpeted in plush, deep blue. The elaborately carved doors at the top of the stairs bore Egyptian figures with upraised swords.

The Shadow didn't bother to knock.

The carved doors opened on an eight-foot-wide gap in a ring of stately columns, which led directly to the mosaic ostentation of the Moonlight Café's seemingly sunken, circular dance floor. The rest of the room described a circle as well, its curving walls softened by sweeps of shimmering gold curtains. The lights of New York sparkled behind an arc of floor-to-ceiling windows that made up the north wall.

The Shadow surged through the gap onto the inlaid dance floor. Shiwan Khan, calmly enthroned under a semicircle of canopy, was alone and obviously expecting him. Nearly centered in room, the bomb hung like a silver Christmas tree ornament.

The Shadow lost no time in setting Khan straight on the seriousness of the situation. His sheathed hands disappeared beneath his cloak, only to reappear a split second later crammed full of pearl-handled retribution.

"The luck of criminals never endures for long," he told Khan.

But if Shiwan Khan was at all troubled by the sight of the guns, his expression didn't betray it. In fact, the city's latest czar of crime and mayhem was actually smiling. Simultaneous with the easy squeeze of The Shadow's trigger fingers, Khan raised his right hand in a twirling gesture, and The Shadow was thrown wildly off balance. The Shadow's first volley of magnum rounds shattered the papyrus-headed, ormolu torchieres that flanked Khan's high-backed chair, but not one touched him. Khan twirled his fingers again as The Shadow was righting himself and firing. Chunks of gilded wood were blasted from the arms and legs of the throne, but Khan remained untouched. And—upright in the chair—laughing gleefully, and waving away gunsmoke.

Intent on emptying them into his rival, The Shadow stiff-armed the guns, only to find himself flat on his back an instant later.

Khan slapped his knees, then positioned his hands as if they were holding a small steering wheel. A counterclockwise turn of the imaginary wheel sent the floor tilting and The Shadow sprawling, the twin automatics sliding out of reach on the acute incline Khan had summoned. When he could manage a glance, The Shadow saw Khan weeping with mirth, extending his hands, as if to be shackled, in a false gesture of surrender.

"Welcome to my funhouse, Ying Ko," Khan told him. "The floor was built to entertain the hotel's late-night revelers. But I seem to have found a better use for it."

The Shadow got up on one knee, preparing to launch himself across the room. But, again, Khan anticipated him. Somber suddenly, Khan gestured sharply to something off to the right of the throne. The Shadow followed Khan's finger to a low table, on top of which rested Marpa Tulku's *phurba*. Khan's hand made a beckoning motion, and the *phurba* began to stir.

The Shadow watched as the dagger with a mind of its own levitated from its stand and rocketed toward him.

20 Reawakenings

The triple-bladed knife interrupted its flight momentarily to hover in midair, inches from his head; then the *phurba* folded itself into an L, so that the face carved into its knobby handle could show The Shadow a look of loathsome recognition.

The Shadow's gloved hand flew for the hilt, but the knife quickly leapt from his grip and began bucking and feinting, aiming first for his arms, then his thighs, then jabbing for his face. The Shadow ducked and the knife spiraled past him, glancing off a column and turning end over end before positioning itself for another run.

The Shadow threw himself to one side as it swooped down on him, catching and tearing a piece from the cloak. Toppled by a sudden tilting of the floor, The Shadow was a second too late in fending off the dagger's follow-up attack on his face. Snarling viciously, it dove for him while he was still tumbling, slicing open his left cheek. The Shadow crab-walked sideways as the blade struck at his hands and feet, then speared for his groin.

The Shadow dropped himself into a sitting posture and spread his legs wide. The knife hit the floor between his legs and tore another piece from the cloak. It skidded backward on its tip, then propelled itself into the air, rotating and twisting, and nosedived for its target, slicing The Shadow's right cheek.

The Shadow saw it drawing a bead on his groin once more, only this time he was ready for it: no sooner did it strike the floor than he had both hands wrapped around the hilt, the upper hand crushed on the head itself, clamping its jaws shut. Bringing all the strength of his powerful arms to bear, he managed to reangle the dagger so that it was pointing more or less at its still enthroned master.

But for all his effort, The Shadow only succeeded in further angering the possessed knife. Now when it rocketed across the room, it took him along for the ride, slamming him into a column, launching him toward the ceiling, stripping him of his signature hat. . . .

Shiwan Khan was at the edge of his seat, observing the contest with mounting disillusionment. When he spoke, his disgust was evident. "Look at you," he told The Shadow. "You're not even capable of controlling yourself, much less the *phurba*."

The knife had him backed to the wall, its tip pressed an eighth-inch into the flesh of his neck. The ebbing strength of The Shadow's hands was all that prevented it from fully slitting his throat. Blood running from the wounds in his cheeks and the slowly elongating wound the dagger was etching into his neck, The Shadow was practically eye to eye with the dagger's scowling face.

Forcing an exhale of disappointment, Khan shrugged off his beaded robe, rose, and stepped down onto the slowly revolving dance floor.

Hearing him approach, The Shadow closed his eyes and took himself back to Tibet—not to the palace of Ying Ko, the poppy fields over which he had presided, the bloody wars with rival chieftains—but to the Temple of the Cobras and to the apprenticeship he had served there.

Khan was wrong: Ying Ko *had* learned to control the *phurba*. But the passive, yin state in which control was achieved had become a stranger to him. Magic and sorcery had little place in the two-fisted, gun-blazing world of vengeful derring-do, where physical prowess mattered above all. That didn't mean, though, that The Shadow couldn't find his way to that calm center again.

Across the room, Khan halted, seeming to sense in The Shadow's sudden composure what was occurring. "What are you up to now, Ying Ko?" he started to say, as The Shadow's hands loosened their hold on the dagger.

And by then it was too late. The *phurba* hung suspended for a moment; then it moved away from The Shadow's neck, gathering speed as it flew, tumbling across the room, and thrust itself deep into the left side of Shiwan Khan's abdomen.

Wide-eyed and gasping in agony, Khan staggered backward.

For almost an hour, Margo and Shrevnitz had been standing in teeming rain, waiting for something to happen. They were under the awning of a luncheonette across the street from the vacant lot but had their umbrellas open just the same. Shrevnitz was holding a book entitled *How to Improve Your Psychic Ability*, a sequel to the one he figured he had already mastered.

"You know what I love about this job, Miss Lane?" he said. "The excitement."

Margo nodded without taking her eyes from the lot.

That Shiwan Khan had hypnotized the entire city into believing that the Hotel Monolith had been torn down was one thing, but it was quite another that the raindrops themselves seemed to be ignoring the building. Shouldn't it look like someone had opened a huge, invisible umbrella above the lot? Magic operated by different rules, she decided.

"Shrevvy, we're staring at a vacant lot," she said, heaving a sigh of sodden bafflement. She turned her head to look at him. "We're standing here in the rain, staring at a vacant lot."

Shrevnitz shrugged, as if to say that it was all part of the job.

And all at once their patience was rewarded.

Concurrent with Khan's stabbing, the citywide spell began to lift, revealing the Hotel Monolith in all its glory. White, with vertical stripes of blue-glaze tiling, a shimmering example of what had been termed "Industrial Moderne," it soared twelve stories to a tall, cylindrical crown, which itself was capped by a 360-degree frieze of naturalistic arabesque. Any sense of squatness was mitigated by symmetrical setbacks at three-story intervals; and central to the facade stood a two-story-tall mythological figure with outstretched wings.

Margo's mouth had dropped open. "That's what he saw! It's unbelievable!"

For blocks in every direction, pedestrians braving the storm were voicing similar exclamations, gesturing in arrant disbelief to the structure that had suddenly sprung up in their midst. Taxicabs and other vehicles slid out of control on the wet streets, slamming into light poles, mailboxes, and one another. With the city under a threat of imminent death by an Asian madman, was the building's appearance a sign of the end—a kind of precatastrophe mass hallucination?

Margo and Shrevnitz hurried into the street, weaving their way through a jumble of cars and their stunned occupants. The hackie made a quick side trip to the Cord for a crowbar, which he used to snap the lock from the fence gate. Then he and Margo dashed across a mud-slicked marble apron for the hotel's triple set of front doors.

In the throne room, struggling to rally from their wounds, Shiwan Khan and The Shadow eyed each other across the tottering, counterclockwising floor. Khan was certainly the worse off, and yet he managed to yank the *phurba* from his body and release a roar that blew out all the glass in the curving north wall. The sky fulminated. Rain and wind whipped at potted palms and ferns that sat by the floor-to-ceiling windows.

The bloody dagger in hand, Khan staggered across the dance floor and up the few stairs to one of the columns. Supporting himself there for a moment, he angled for a section of the east wall, where gold silk curtained the entrance to his meditation chamber.

The Shadow got to his feet and followed, nourishing one of the retrieved magnums with a fresh clip. He raised the weapon and ripped the curtains to one side. But instead of finding his adversary or some secret exit, there was only a towering, upright coffin—the silver coffin of Temüjin, which Khan's henchmen had stolen from the Museum of Art and Antiquity a day earlier.

The Shadow dropped what was left of his cloak and undid the five dragon's-foot latches that secured the coffin's sculpted doors. Throwing them open, he shoved the automatic forward. But the coffin, too, was empty.

Cautiously, he began to run his hand over the moiré inner lining. Then, finding nothing peculiar, he stepped inside, ultimately allowing the doors to close behind him. Something clicked in the dark, and the bottom panel of the coffin gave way.

Wounded, Khan had lost his hold on Reinhardt Lane as well.

The professor came to his senses in what he quickly recognized was an expensive hotel room—though he couldn't for the life of him recall how he had gotten there. The lamps on either side of the double bed were on, and he was standing fully dressed, opposite a wall mirror centered over the couch. Gazing out the window, he determined that he was at least ten stories above the streets of Manhattan's Lower East Side.

He went to the door and peeked into a lighted hall-way, elegantly decorated, with gray carpeting, and antique chairs, canopies, and commodes. The odd thing was, he seemed to be the floor's sole guest.

Three minutes and four flights of stairs later, he was even more bewildered to run into Margo, who was hurrying down a hallway, accompanied by a man wearing a peacoat and green corduroys. She rushed into his arms and hugged him.

"Margo, where are we?" Lane asked in obvious distress. "Please, tell me what's going on."

Margo took hold of his hand. "Well, see, there's this guy, Shiwan Khan—" She stopped herself and swung to the unidentified man. "Shrevvy, you better go for the police."

The man nodded and ran off. Lane gazed at his daughter in consternation.

"Dad, the whole story's going to have to wait until later," she told him. "But in the meantime, there's something you've got to do—right now."

Lane shook his head. "Do about what, dear?"

"About the atom bomb!"

The Shadow made a soft landing. He calculated that he hadn't fallen more than thirty feet, and the fall seemed to have delivered him into an outsize laundry bin. Overhead was what could have been a laundry chute—three chutes, in fact, each with its own heap of delivered goods. On closer inspection, however, he realized that he hadn't dropped onto soiled clothing, bedding, or tablecloths, but onto scraps of fabric and carpet remnants apparently pitched down the chutes during final construction of the Moonlight Café.

The Shadow scrambled down off the pile and planted his feet on the floor. His cat's eyes made sufficient use of the dim light to define his immediate surroundings: the room was round and approximated the dimensions of Khan's throne room. He reasoned that he was still within the Monolith's cylindrical crown, possibly directly beneath the dance floor. Indeed, he could hear the humming of the complex mechanism that governed the floor's spin and pitch.

The Shadow backhanded blood from one cheek and adjusted his hold on the handgun's nacre grip. Ahead of him lay an assortment of objects he didn't identify as tables until he was almost on top of them. There had to be at least sixty of them, assembled or in parts, scattered about, stacked up, leaning against one another.

Further along were chairs, in pretty much the same state of disarray. Next came the pieces of a portable stage, column bases and capitals, lengths of hardwood flooring and arcs of treading for the stairs that surrounded the dance floor, curtain rods, fabric-wrapped cornices, panes of window glass, even bedframes, mattresses, and mirrors. The Shadow felt as if he were maneuvering his way through the world's largest attic.

But neither sign nor sound of Shiwan Khan, only the wavering hum of electric motors and a gentle whirring of gears.

A few minutes of stalking delivered The Shadow into an aisle formed by a palisade of tall, brocaded curtains and a domino arrangement of full-length mirrors—some of them in freestanding frames; others of the sort typically found affixed to the backs of bathroom doors. At the end of the aisle, remote light gleamed from a faintly reflective surface.

Into which Khan suddenly stepped.

As if unbidden, The Shadow's automatic spoke, and Khan's image splintered, as The Shadow's own had on the night Margo Lane had been sent to kill him.

The Shadow quickly determined where Khan must have been standing for his reflection to have appeared.

A violent sweep of his left hand parted the curtains, and he stepped through them into a veritable hall of mirrors: cheval glasses, girandoles, trumeaux, and wall mirrors standing on end. Manifold images of the would-be ruler of the free world were on hand to applaud The Shadow's entrance. Concealed lights came up and Khan's image moved, disappearing from one group of mirrors only to appear in another. The Shadow pivoted, hoping to suss out Khan's true position, the magnum eager to speak.

Then, from behind him, Khan materialized, flesh and bone and wailing a Mongol battle cry as he charged, slashing for The Shadow with the raised *phurba*.

The Shadow lurched to one side, but not nimbly enough to avoid the tapering, three-sided blade.

In the throne room, Reinhardt Lane was marveling at the suspended sphere that spelled doom for the city. In the hearts of the timer-display vacuum tubes glowed the numerals 1, 1, 1, 2, 6: one hour, eleven minutes, twenty-six seconds.

And counting.

"This is really most impressive," he said to Margo. "Most impressive, indeed. Who built it?"

"You did," she told him in a rush. This, despite the fact that it was the professor, in a dazed state, who had led them to the site of the bomb. "Now *un*build it!"

Lane was perplexed. "*I* built this?" He produced a pair of oval, wire-rim spectacles from the breast pocket of his jacket and slipped them on over the pair he was already wearing.

"Yes, Dad. So I'm sure you can deactivate it. If you'd only—"

"But just look at the craftsmanship."

"Dad!" Margo yelled, taking hold of his shoulders and shaking him.

The ceremonial knife The Shadow thought he had tamed had sliced through his double-breasted coat, his shirt, and the skin of his chest. Khan was back to his funhouse tricks, his reflection shifting from one array of mirrors to the next. But The Shadow was still gunning for him.

"Come no further, Ying Ko," Khan cautioned. "This is not an arena you wish to venture into."

His usual risibility quieted, The Shadow ignored the warning, snaking his way through aisle after reflective aisle in an effort to close in on Khan's voice. For all the maneuvering, however, The Shadow seemed to be getting nowhere fast. In fact, Khan actually appeared to be receding from view.

The Shadow came to a halt, thwarted vindication oozing from him. Khan's reflections were undergoing a transformation; in their stead were resolving images of The Shadow himself—save that they belonged to an earlier incarnation. . . .

To Ying Ko: who had brought destruction of many a highland village; who had laid siege to the sacrosanct Potola itself; who had dealt death to the cities of the United States and Europe; who had calmly ordered the execution of his trusted friend and adviser, Wu, merely to send a message to his competitors in the opium trade.

"Gaze into your past, Ying Ko," Khan was saying. "Behold your former self, your true shadow, and tell me again why you refuse to become my willing ally in evil."

Professor Lane muttered to himself while he labored to deactivate the timer. "Cut this wire, isolate this relay, reroute this circuit. . . ." With a snip, he cut one wire and turned his attention to another.

Working with arms raised over his head, he had unscrewed and removed the timer's curved access panel, which he had stowed in his jacket pocket. Tucked into the nacelle behind the panel was a wiring board composed of sixteen pairs of slot-head screws. The board was nested in a tangle of copper wires, sheathed in red, green, yellow, and blue braided cloth.

Margo, who had taken off her wool coat, was pacing nervously behind him, on what seemed to be a very unsteady floor, stopping every so often to monitor her father's progress. Just now she heard the snap of his wire cutters and glanced at the timer display, gasping when she saw that the seconds and minutes were passing in a blur.

Fifty minutes, forty, thirty ...

"Dad!" she screamed.

He angled his head away from the sphere to regard the glass panel, which was suddenly displaying single digits: *ten minutes, nine, eight ...*

"Oh, dear me," Lane said.

Frantically, he spliced the wire he had cut only a moment earlier, and the timer resumed a normal countdown.

With only four minutes and seven seconds remaining to detonation.

21 Rolling Thunder

Depictions of his violent past continued to play across the dazzling faces of the mirrors—as they had so often in his mind's eye: the beatings he endured and dished out as a youth; the vengeance he extracted on those who had dared to dishonor him: the viciousness he unleashed against a jealous cousin; the myriad sanctioned crimes he committed during the war; the bloody turf battles that were the order of the day in the Himalaya and the Hindu Kush; the redirected rage The Shadow brought to the city; the identity hoax he had perpetrated on the world; the dread he had induced in Margo Lane. . . .

The images were never far from his thoughts. But now, to see them exteriorized was almost more than he could stand. The human in him sought to deny the truth, while the beast reveled.

Khan made good use of The Shadow's inner struggle. His reflection streaking across the mirrors, Khan materialized within arm's reach of his quarry.

More, within blade's reach.

A leather-clad hand rose to stave off Khan's overhand blow, and was pierced through its palm. The Shadow raged against the pain as Khan reared for a second attack. The Shadow's other hand came up, only to be similarly impaled.

Bleeding profusely, The Shadow collapsed on hands and knees, snarling like a cornered animal.

Reinhardt Lane's wire cutters severed a red-to-red connection.

Margo—standing off to one side of the dangling bomb, fingertips to her mouth—heard a worrisome *click!*, and looked up in time to see the hook that attached the sphere to the cable open.

"Wrong, again," the scientist said, as the sphere disengaged.

It hit the circular floor with a hollow clang and rolled toward the perimeter below the throne, sending the floor into a sudden tilt. Lane pitched over sideways, tipping the floor in the opposite direction, and Margo's feet came out from under her. The sphere struck the carpeted edge of the concentric ring of stairs and caromed at an acute angle, setting the floor rotating as well as tipping. The Lanes scrambled to their feet, fell once more, then rose and began to make desperate lunges for the sphere as it was rebounding off the stairs and pinballing around the floor. The physicist almost succeeded in stopping it, but it rolled from his grasp, dropping him on his face. Margo was just getting up when the sphere bowled her over on its way back from the stairs.

"This is impossible," Reinhardt told his daughter. "I can't even stay on my feet!"

Margo, sprawled on the floor with her blue dress twisted around her, threw him a piqued look. "Yeah, well, try doing it in *heels*!"

The sphere kept striking and banking like some outsize billiard ball for what felt like ten minutes—though Margo was relieved to note—when she happened to catch a glimpse of the timer—that only a minute had elapsed. Just then, however, the floor tipped southward and the bomb rolled through the gap in the columned ring. Reinhardt had just about reached it when it shot between the Egyptian-figured doors and went tumbling down the stairs into the hallway.

Margo recalled that the display had shown three minutes remaining before detonation.

Weakened but back on his feet and eager for revenge, he asked himself why Shiwan Khan hadn't finished the job. Did Khan still expect that they could forge a partnership?

Reading The Shadow's thoughts, the villainous Asian suddenly manifested in the mirrors.

"Poor Ying Ko," he said, with false sincerity. "You never could decide who or what you were. But now, Shiwan Khan will decide for you." He raised the *phurba* over his head. "You will be *nothing*. I'm sick of you. I'm sick of both of us."

The Shadow reached deeply into himself, draining the reservoir of his contained power. Veins leapt out in his taut neck and forehead; his face rippled and bulged. Blood seeped from one eye, then the other, coursing down over his ax-keen nose and throbbing cheeks. The object of his concentrated will—the room and its hundreds of mirrors—began to quake.

Khan eyed him with misgiving. Then, grasping that he had a time bomb of his own to disarm, Khan commanded The Shadow to stop. But the rumbling only increased.

The bomb thundered down the hallway, glancing off wainscotting and chairs, with the Lanes chasing after it.

As if set on escaping, the sphere overturned tables and lamps—all of which the Lanes were forced to hurdle—then found its way to the stairway to the floor below.

Having taken several nasty falls on the dance floor, the professor had to be helped along by his daughter, who, quite unnecessarily, felt the need to urge him on. The two were only fifty feet behind the sphere when it rolled down the stairs, but Reinhardt's limp slowed them considerably, so that by the time they reached the lower floor they no longer had the object in sight.

Although they could hear the bomb banging into furniture along its route.

Margo hurried around a bend in the hallway, then paused briefly at the top of another stairway to listen for sounds of damage. Hearing nothing in the carpeted hallway ahead, she concluded that the sphere had again found the stairs, and she and her father descended to the next floor.

They were rushing down a stretch of carpeted hallway when the professor heard a rumbling noise overhead. "It's upstairs!" he exclaimed.

At the end of the hallway they came to a stairway that accessed the upper floor. The stairway curved around to the right in its ascent and was bordered below by a small garden of ferns and palms in earthenware pots. Side by side, the Lanes climbed, but they stopped short of the top when a threatening shadow appeared on the curved wall to their left—rounded and fast increasing in size.

The sphere rolled into view above them and came bumping down the stairs, sending Reinhardt front-flipping over the brass banister into the plants, and Margo rolling down the stairs to the floor. The sphere

missed her by inches when it hit the hallway's gray run-
ner, its momentum carrying it directly toward the hotel's sole elevator shaft. No car was visible, but the
shaft was obstructed by only a retractable gate.

A somewhat shaken Dr. Lane was peering from between parted palm fronds when the sphere crashed
forcefully into and flattened the gate, beyond which lay
an eleven-story plunge to the lobby.

Strident discord shook the mirrored space where
Shiwan Khan and The Shadow were faced off in a
Manichean showdown. Amplified to an unbearable de-
gree by the room's circular design, the dissonance grew
louder and louder until it was suddenly surpassed by
another: the sound of shattering glass.

Khan hurled himself to the floor as the mirrors fragmented, as if struck by wrecking balls. Shards of sliv-
ered glass ripped through the room, launching for the
ceiling, swooping and cycloning. . . . Jagged edges
sliced at arms, legs, and face. One particularly willful
piece left a deep, red furrow across the back of The
Shadow's neck; others spiraled around Khan.

The two were slowly being cut to ribbons.

All the while, The Shadow had been scanning for the
single, most bloodthirsty shard of the swarm and, now
having located that one, he was giving it his undivided
attention. It was a long, slender piece that tapered to a
sharp tip, already speckled with The Shadow's own
blood. Seemingly placid amid the frenzy, it was hovering not far from where The Shadow knelt, readying
itself for guided flight.

Shiwan Khan spied the deviant shard and screamed—
unintentionally enabling it. Fully tasked and targeted, it

streaked across the hall and buried itself three inches deep into the right side of his forehead, driving him backward to the floor.

The Shadow waited a moment, then got up and went over to him, a triumphant laugh already escaping him.

Knocked flat by the sphere, the elevator gate was horizontally wedged in the shaft with the bomb sitting on top of it. The Lancs had tested the soundness of the gate before putting their weight on it, but no sooner had they crawled onto it than it had altered its lie, dropping three feet before coming to a solid rest.

Margo's heart was pounding in her ears. Not only from the gate's sudden shift, but from the vertigo that had gripped her when she had chanced to look down the dimly lighted shaft.

The sphere had ended its journey with the timer and display pressed against the rear wall of the shaft. Wire cutters in hand, Dr. Lane was bent over the bomb, struggling to disable the final relays. Margo crouched beside him, shivering in the cold updraft, her eyes glued to the upside-down display, which was counting down from thirteen seconds.

All at once her father's hand began to falter. "I don't know which wire Farley ran to the timer and which one he ran to the implosion detonator." The wire cutters were poised over a maze of fabric-sheathed, copper wiring, in which two stood out: one red, one green. He looked at Margo. "I just don't know."

"Choose!" she screamed at him.

The numeral filaments in the vacuum tubes showed 0, 0, 0, 1, 0.

"Hurry!"

Lane showed his daughter a determined look; then he positioned the jaws of the cutters around one of the wires. "It has to be this green one."

Margo followed his gaze—*to a red wire*!

The timer was counting down from five seconds when her left hand shot out to restrain her father's hand. At the same time, her right yanked at the green wire, but the damn thing was fastened beneath one of the wiring board's slot-head screws!

Finally, she managed to get her entire hand on the wire and she tugged. The wire snapped at the screw head and came free in her hand.

In the depths of the vacuum tube furthest to the right, a red 1 glowed.

Spent, Margo collapsed atop the defused bomb and regarded her father with weary disbelief. She pointed to the wire she had disconnected, then the one he had almost severed. "*This* is green," she said. "*That's* red."

Lane sagged against the beryllium sphere. "Not to these old eyes."

The storm had abated. But what with the knot of black-and-whites, yellow cabs, and interlocked delivery wagons and trucks, the scene outside the reappeared Hotel Monolith was chaotic.

Police Commissioner Barth, wearing a trenchcoat and a new fedora, worked his way through an astonished throng of policemen, fireman, and onlookers. Just inside the gated entrance to what only an hour before had been a vacant lot, he stopped to gape at the building, removed his hat, then putting it back on. He was staring at the structure's winged figure when he observed Margo Lane and an elderly professorial type exit through the front doors. Surmising that the man was Lane's missing father, he signaled to a police lieutenant that the couple should be brought to him.

"What in the world has been going on in there, Miss Lane?" he asked when she arrived. "And where did this building *come* from?" Before she could even respond, his expression turned hard and suspicious. "I know this has something to do with Shiwan Khan's threat to blow up the city. But I want the full truth: was that maniac The Shadow involved in this?"

Margo gave him her best glare. "The Shadow is hardly a maniac, Commissioner. In fact, The Shadow is—"

She caught sight of Moe Shrevnitz standing at the edge of the crowd and bit back her words. As their eyes met, the hackie gave his head a slow side-to-side shake, and he pressed his forefinger to his lips. Then he winked and backed into the crowd, disappearing from sight.

Barth had swung around to follow her gaze, but now he was eyeing her once more. "You were about to tell me something about The Shadow, Miss Lane. The Shadow is *what*, precisely?"

She looked at him and smiled thinly. "A myth, Commissioner. Only a myth." She put her arm around her father's waist, and they began to move off.

Barth's face fell. Covertly, he took a flask from the inner pocket of his trenchcoat and took a quick swig. He knew that Margo Lane was lying. But he decided that it was more comforting to take her at her word than to believe otherwise.

THE SHADOW

tacked infidel with pens in his bony pocket were die.
for this brown.

22 Inmates

Shiwan Khan, vaunted descendant of the Ruler of All Peoples Living in Felt Tents and present landlord of the subterranean Mongolian city of Xanadu, on the shores of the sacred river Alph, awoke from what seemed a dream in which his arms had been pulled from their sockets by teams of wild horses.

He found it curious, however, that even in the waking world he couldn't move his limbs.

His eyes—sunken, rimmed with red, and a shade paler than they had been a week earlier—snapped open and surveyed his surroundings: the padded, white walls of his tiny room, the narrow cot that was the room's sole piece of furniture, the straightjacket that lashed his arms to his body. . . .

He waged a brief but futile struggle against the jacket's three leather belts. Then he looked behind him, hoping that his eyes had missed something during their initial survey of the room. Centered in the rear wall was a small, barred window.

The door to his cell opened while he had his back to it. Turning, Khan watched a bald man enter, carrying a tray that held a bowl of broth. Attired in white trousers and a white jacket, the man didn't strike Khan as an attendant or an aide. He suspected that this bespectacled infidel with pens in his breast pocket was a doctor of some sort.

"You," he intoned, in his command voice. "Look at me. Look deep into the eyes of Kha Khan."

The doctor set the tray down on the foot of the bed and did as he had been commanded though Khan seemed to detect a hint of something disingenuous in the man's expression.

"Release me at once," Khan told him

The doctor actually *laughed*, humoring him.

"Now, now, we'll have none of that, Mr. Khan."

Worse, the doctor laid his hands on the right side of Khan's head, which had obviously been shaved from crown to ear. "Let's just have a look at those stitches, shall we?"

Khan scowled at him. "Stitches? What have you heathens done to me?"

"Saved your life, I suspect."

The doctor's fingers probed what Khan understood to be a circle of large sutures, a good two inches in diameter.

"We were forced to excise a small portion of the frontal lobe of your brain," the doctor was saying. "But, believe me, you won't miss it. It's a part that no one uses—unless of course if you happen to be a practitioner of telepathy." He laughed, and continued laughing all the way to the door.

Khan began to explore his own mind, his eyes widening with horror. "Wait!" he screamed. "You can't leave me like this!"

But the doctor simply whistled to himself as he closed the door behind him. In his final glimpse of him, Khan noticed a familiar red ring adorning the third finger of the man's right hand.

Khan rose from the cot and stumbled to the door, pressing his face against a window covered with wire mesh. "You can't do this to me! I am the descendant of Temüjin himself—Genghis Khan!"

He gazed into a starkly lighted corridor with blue-white walls, where doctors with pointed white beards were blithely going about their business, and orderlies were minding patients strapped into wooden wheel-chairs with caned backrests.

"I am the descendant of Genghis Khan!" Khan repeated.

He listened for a moment, certain that his declaration would bring someone scurrying to him. But, instead, all he heard was the voice of someone in an adjoining cell.

"*I* am the descendant of Genghis Khan," a man said.

"No, *I* am," yelled a second man.

"The hell you are! *I* am!" said a third.

Soon, the declaration had been taken up by every inmate within earshot—an asylumful of Shiwan Khans.

Though now only one of them was screaming in panic—and for dreams of conquest unfulfilled.

Lamont Cranston and Margo Lane were a handsome couple; he, in black overcoat and homburg; she, in a fur-trimmed jacket and matching hat. People they passed on the sidewalks of Times Square regarded them with a mix of envy and admiration. Made for each other, some surely told themselves.

Minutes earlier they had stopped to observe a game of three-card monte, where an obvious out-of-towner had been in danger of losing the farm in his efforts to choose the upside-down "lady"—the elusive red queen—rather than either of the two black tens she was partnered with. While Cranston and Margo watched, the man surrendered close to five hundred dollars to the swift-handed dealer, whom Cranston had spotted as a sharp. When, despite entreaties from his wife, the man had laid his watch, his wife's wedding ring, and the remainder of his cash on the dealer's milk crate, Cranston had intervened. Not in a physical way, but by discerning something about the dealer's technique which he then wordlessly conveyed to the bettor.

The dealer and his shill's dismayed incredulity was palpable when the man selected the right card. Winning *big* . . .

"I still don't understand," Margo said while they were walking away. "I was sure the queen had a bent corner when the cards were being shuffled. But then when that man finally found the queen, it was one of the tens whose corner was bent."

"A Mexican turnover," Cranston explained. "The dealer straightened the queen's corner and crimped the ten while he executed his hype—his overthrow move—that landed the queen in the middle, when it seemed as though it should have been on the right."

"You got that by reading the dealer's mind?"

"I didn't have to. But I did offer a suggestion to the dealer's intended victim."

"I didn't hear you offer anything."

"Maybe you just weren't paying attention," he said.

Margo remained silent for the next couple of blocks.

"I'm ravenous," Cranston said. "Where should we eat?"

Margo rocked her head from side to side. "How about that Chinese restaurant you took me to the night we met?"

Knowing that he was being teased, Cranston cut her a look. "What would you say to Italian this time?"

She smiled and was about to agree when Cranston suddenly stopped at the entrance to a brick alley, bordered on one side by a dealer in second-hand jewelry and on the other by an embalmer's. She understood that it was the alley they had been headed for on the day she had told him about Farley Claymore and Mari-Tech—the alley that led to The Shadow's hidden sanctum.

Margo put a hand on Cranston's arm as if to restrain him. "Lamont, even The Shadow needs to take a holiday. Shiwan Khan isn't a threat anymore. You won, and the world's safe from madmen who want to rule it."

He looked at her uncertainly. "Is it?"

"Of course, it is." She brightened for his benefit. "After all, Lamont, this is the twentieth century."

He frowned dubiously. "Who knows what evil lurks in the hearts of men, Margo?"

"You tell me."

They locked eyes and kissed, deeply and lingeringly. But while she was exiting his embrace, she felt him slip a ring onto the third finger of her left hand. Margo stared at the ruby-red oval, then at Cranston's own. She wanted to ask him if the ring was being given by The Shadow or by Lamont Cranston, but she never got the chance.

Cranston's ring had began to pulsate, as if in dire warning, and he was already turning away from her. She followed him a few steps into the alley, then stopped when he did.

"If needed, you will receive instructions," he said.

She shook her head in sudden confusion. "But suppose I'm not home, suppose I'm out somewhere. How will you know where to find me."

"I'll know," he told her, and was gone.